QUEERS IN KILTS

www.sincyrpublishing.com
sincyr.submissions@gmail.com

Edited by Sienna Saint-Cyr

Print ISBN: 978-1-948780-22-3

CONTENTS

HOW I REALLY MET MY WIFE

by Raven Sky

WE ALL HAD DIFFERENT REASONS for being in that room. There were the ready, polished excuses we offered to others and then murkier motivations too. We believed our excuses with varying degrees of naiveté and denial. But whatever brought us there, there we were: Jake, naked on the futon, clearly excited, Monique, trembling visibly in attractive uncertainty, and me, Alex, jaded at only twenty-five, leading the show in my lingerie.

These were not our real names. But then nothing that happened in that room was ever real for me. Until she came along.

My wife and I can never tell people the truth of how me met, so we lie. We agreed long ago on an acceptably cute and romantic tale that would fit with the mainstream, middle class, suburban life that we live today. Because everyone knows that happy families don't begin in erotic massage parlors.

Except that ours did.

The best lies contain a kernel of pure truth, so let me share with you—as we did with anyone who knew our secret—the lies that we told about why we were there. I was a university student, the first in my family to attend, and I was finishing up a very expensive degree. She was a newly single young mother, looking to make money to fight for sole custody of her daughter. He was an arrogant prick cheating on his wife. Okay, so that's not fair, but neither was what he was doing. Though I was hardly in a position to judge—not that it stopped me.

Jake was one of my regulars. I didn't have a lot of them because I refused to string men along with flirty suggestions that maybe more might happen between us in time if we got close enough. I wasn't into having a work boyfriend who would buy me gifts and ask me about my real life. This was all business for me and I was totally upfront and in charge. That was part of the appeal: that I could boss men around and feel like I was taking advantage of them for once.

Jake stuck with me though, because he was, as mentioned previously, an arrogant prick. He was young to be frequenting a massage parlor, and he was ridiculously hot, and he knew it. He walked into the place like he expected all of us to catfight and claw each other's eyes out over the chance to touch his naked flesh. I suspect he picked me precisely because I seemed supremely uninterested.

Men don't expect to find lesbians working in a "rub-and-tug." But men don't gross me out; they just don't turn me on. I know plenty of my Sapphic sisters would balk at the idea of giving a guy the standard "happy ending" hand-job to finish off an erotic massage, but it was never a big deal for me. I'd run my hands along their body, wriggling in my lingerie in what I judged to be an appealingly sensual manner. They'd feel up my tits and beg to feel more. I'd refuse in a firm but flirty way.

If they were regulars, and I knew that they would respect my boundaries, I'd give them a good view of my pussy, straddling their face, and keeping it just out of reach. If they were new, I'd simply lay with them, continuing the whole sensual wriggling thing before the standard ending: the jacking of their cock. They'd come and I'd make a bunch of money. That's how it worked. That was the routine. It was almost robotic for me, after the first month. Honestly, in my mind, I was usually reviewing things I needed to remember for the next exam. I was never wet. I was never tempted to do more. At least not with the clients, but with my co-workers…well, that was another story.

The moment Jenny stepped through the door of Taboo, my heart inexplicably clenched. It sounds like another lie, but I swear it's true. She looked so lost and out of place, and yet was putting on a fiercely brave front that was only betrayed by the wild gleam of her eyes and the way every action she took was jerky, as if she was holding back and then pushing herself to overcome the resistance. Every girl in the place was giving her an immediate, calculated once-over. How pretty was she?

How threatening? Which clients would go to her now? Would she get along or be a bitch? She was a petite little blonde thing with dark, keen brown eyes. She struck me right away as a small and perhaps adrift, but formidably determined woman. I wanted to know her and her story from the very beginning. Luckily, my manager was a lazy party girl who managed nothing more than snorting coke and passing off her minor work responsibilities to me. She decided that I should train Jenny the next day.

Jenny decided to go by Monique, which seemed all wrong to me. I didn't think she could pull the name off. Monique sounded sophisticated and street-smart, whereas this girl, for all her feisty resolve, seemed pretty naïve. But maybe our work names were all aspirational. I picked Alex because it was gender-neutral enough to sound strong. I didn't want clients thinking they could get away with anything and the name was a kind of warning that I would not be a touchy-feely, giggly, silly girl.

We opened around noon and I walked "Monique" through the routines. She listened attentively and nodded. If she was panicking, she managed to hide it. I'm not sure I hid my desire as well as she hid her fear. Monique wore a cute schoolgirl kilt with a rather transparent white blouse that showed off the black bra beneath it. I'd seen my coworkers try to pull off the sexy schoolgirl look before, but never this successfully. Jenny embodied the unnerving, paradoxical mixture of coquettish innocence and sultry cunning that whispered Lolita for anyone attuned to that particular kink. Maybe that's what drew me to her too. The enigma of her contradictory vulnerability and strength.

It was pretty dead that afternoon, so we were able to talk for a long time. Most of the other girls spent any dead time watching the little TV in the waiting area, but I usually spent my time studying. That day, I studied Jenny. I was a pretty good student, but damn, if I had studied for my classes the way I studied her face and words, I would have earned enough scholarship money to quit this stupid job. Her skirt was ridiculously short. Its pleats swayed in time with her bottom every time she got up to go anywhere and I swear I caught the briefest glimpse of ass cleavage once or twice. How could I not be bewitched? My fingers ached to inch up her thighs beneath that little red kilt and discover the secrets it hid. Of course my mind filled up with ludicrous, clichéd fantasies of taking her over my knee and punishing her for her too-short skirt. Making her stand at attention and measuring her hemline to her finger lengths drawn out along her pale, quivering thigh. It was hard to concentrate on reality when her outfit inspired such easy fantasy.

She offered her rehearsed excuse right away. "I'm not going to be here for long," she began. "I'm just trying to make some money to fight my ex for sole custody."

"You're a mom?" I asked, surprised, given her age and diminutive stature.

She bristled. "I'm just doing what I've got to do. All I want to do it take my daughter and run away, but I'm stuck in this shithole city until I can prove he doesn't deserve custody."

"I'm not judging," I explained. "Trust me; no one thinks they'll wind up here and no one plans to stay. It's no big deal that you're a mom. A couple of the girls here have kids."

"Yeah, well, like I said, it's just temporary. Until I can save enough for the lawyer."

"Sure."

I didn't know this then, but Jenny can't stand silence. She'll fill it with any kind of inane blather. Perhaps that was why she started sharing about her ex. I certainly wasn't prying enough to ask. Her eyes teared up at one point when she talked about the moment she stopped making excuses and realized her boyfriend was abusive. She excused herself to go to the bathroom then, but we both knew she was really going there to cry in privacy. Before the first client arrived, Jenny had pretty much shared her entire life story, told in a defensive rush. She clearly wasn't at ease with her decision to work there and I found myself wanting to protect her and make her way easier.

I found myself wanting to do other things too. Sometimes while she talked, her words just fell away, and I was left mesmerized, watching the shapes made by her mouth. She had nice teeth. Her lips were a little thin, but I liked the planes of her face. Her eyes were so dark brown that they were almost black. They were also sharp and missed nothing.

"Why are you staring at me?"

"Am I? Sorry. I was just listening."

"No, you weren't. You were staring."

This kind of blunt, direct challenge would be a difficult characteristic of her interactions with me for years. She is the brusque truth-teller in the relationship and I am the tactful diplomat. Both roles have their place, I know, but I really wish she'd learn to soften her edges a bit.

At that time, Jake was always coming to see me directly after work on Fridays. He said it started his weekend off right. He strolled through the door at his usual time, ego and privilege radiating from him as he filled the room at once with his booming voice and macho energy.

"Where's my girl at? Jake needs to start his weekend off right."

I motioned for Jenny to follow me and went to greet Jake, rolling my eyes internally at his annoying habit of speaking of himself in the third person.

"Woah! Who's this new cutie?" Jake bellowed. I watched him turn on the charm even thicker and grab her hand to place a kiss. "Milady," he joked, as though he were a knight and she a damsel in distress.

"This is Jake. Don't let him fool you. He's a dick."

"Alex, I'm shocked and hurt. After all this time, I still haven't convinced you of what a great guy I am? You know, I never have to work this hard with anyone else." He winked and made to manhandle me right there in the lobby, but I evaded him by moving behind the front desk to write down the details of his visit.

"I assume you're looking for the usual today, Jake. Would it be okay if Monique here tags along? I'm training her. There'd be no extra cost to you."

"Two for the price of one, eh? I'd say this is gonna be an amazing weekend," Jake enthused, looking Monique up and down lasciviously.

"Great. You know the drill. Go get undressed and relax and wait for us. We'll be there in a few minutes."

"Okay, but don't take too long, cutie," Jake teased, placing his man paws on Monique's ass and pulling her in close. "I'm excited to see what you've got going on under this little kilt of yours."

"Okay, okay, Jake. Go easy on the new girl, please. Don't scare her off. Get inside," I said, shooing him away.

He sauntered off, whistling to himself and I turned to Jenny to assess how she was doing. She had a concerned look on her face and I began to worry that she might back out. "What's wrong?" I asked.

"He's wearing a wedding ring."

"Yeah. He's a dick. I told you." This didn't seem to reassure her so I kept talking. "Look, that's the deal. Most of them are married, but they've got a million excuses. Their marriage is a sham and they're only staying together for the kids. It's not really cheating because it's not sex. She has no time for him now with the new baby. She got fat. Whatever. I feel badly about their wives, I do, but I'm not the one betraying them. I'm just trying to better my life. And some of the guys are sweet."

She looked dubious so I rushed on, "Seriously. One of my regulars is an amputee who lost his arm in a freak work accident. His girlfriend left him right after it. And you can imagine that it's not exactly easy to date when you're partially dismembered, so he comes here for some human touch and connection. I totally get and respect that. And I really like him. A lot of guys are just lonely and want to be touched. It's a lot easier for women to get touch whenever we want it, right? Honestly, sometimes they pay me just to hold them and talk. It's sad actually. But then there are the married jerks, like Jake too. It's a mixed bag. But that's the job. Think you can you handle it?"

She took a deep breath and seemed to gather herself in tightly. "Yes, let's do this." We went back to the waiting area and began to change into our lingerie. It was all I could do to keep my eyes focused on the floor. I didn't want to freak her out, but I was dying to see what she would wear.

"Is this okay?" she asked, adjusting her boobs in a tight-fitting purple lace negligee. My heart rate sped up and I swallowed self-consciously before nodding my head, not trusting my voice, as my eyes wandered approvingly up and down her compact curves. I took a breath and gathered myself too. I had to get it together and lead this interaction, I reminded myself.

"Okay," I began. "Jake always pays for an hour long reverse. That means we have to stretch things out at least forty-five minutes or he'll complain. The reverse means he gets to 'massage' us too, which is really just code for he can touch us too, but where he touches is completely up to you. Some girls allow them to touch between their legs and some don't. Whatever you decide, you've got to be clear and consistent across the clients, as some of them talk."

"I'd rather not, but will it matter to making money?" she asks, bluntly.

"Yes and no. Obviously the girls who allow it get more clients but they tend to be nasty cheapskates and I don't want them anyway. I'd rather do less work for more pay, you know? Plus you don't know where their hands have been. Or you do actually. Jake's totally playing with himself right now, waiting for us. I'd rather keep it clean and I always just tell them that if I let all the guys touch me there, they wouldn't want to. Most of them don't like being reminded that they share us with others. And they don't want to think about how that could get pretty dirty, you know? On the other hand, some guys revel in that thought, to be honest, but again, they're not the guys I want."

"Okay, got it."

I hesitated before plunging on. "Alright. The other thing is that usually with a double there's a little show the girls put on for the guys. Just kind of making out with each other to get them going. Each girl is different in how far she takes it. Again, it's totally up to you," I finished, literally holding my breath, waiting to see how she would respond.

She pondered a moment, then burst out laughing.

your damn wedding ring before you grab my tits? What the fuck is wrong with you?"

Jake looked at me accusingly but I just laughed. I had no idea she'd play along and up the ante in our tormented dynamic. I found it hilarious and super hot. She was so tiny and he was so huge. It was funny to watch her put him in his place. "I'll let you see my pussy, Jake. You can watch while Alex touches it. You can even come close. But don't you dare touch me. You just touch yourself. And if you're a really good boy, I'll let you come on my tits. Understand?" Jake nodded, mutely and enthusiastically.

She strode back to me then and I believe it's fair to say that I was enamored from that moment forward. I thought she was lost and needed protection? This chick was a force to be reckoned with. How did she ever let some man abuse her? It felt inconceivable. But then I realized that maybe she was working out something about her relationships with men through this job. Just like me, a small voice in my head admitted.

She returned to my side on the bed and kissed me feverishly. Jake crouched by the edge of the futon like some weird outsider.

"Please fuck me," she invited frankly.

I'd never actually had sex with any of the girls at Taboo. It was all a silly show, and I'd only been with two other women before now, so her words both thrilled and terrified me. But I looked down at her beautiful body and something inside me stirred deeply. I wanted to love her more than I'd wanted anything in a long time. I brought my mouth to her curves and lavished attention on them. I kissed, licked, bit, fondled, caressed and squeezed every piece of her that I could, before hesitating at the soft strip of fuzz between her thighs.

"Are you sure?" I asked.

"Show me what I've been missing," she challenged, eyebrow cocked. And I must have done so, because we've been together ever since.

We worked at Taboo for another year and made a killing with our doubles, shamelessly exploiting our sexual connection for shitloads of money. Jenny won custody and I graduated. We quit the industry and moved in together. I had an insta-family, and all in all, through the usual ups and downs, we've made a good life together.

Our beginning is not the fairy-tale story most people are used to hearing, so we don't tell it. We tell an innocuous lie and feel a thrill of transgression run through us with each telling. Holding hands at Little League practice, talking to the other moms. We remember Jake, poor fool. We remember Monique and Alex, and the way that they brought us together. A strange, edgy backstory to our current white picket-fence reality. I look around at the other moms and wonder. Whose husband is feeling up the latest version of Alex and Monique? Who else has secrets as juicy as us? What is real in the façade that we present to each other? But then I look over at my wife, cheering fiercely for our daughter, clumsily rounding the bases, and I remember that the best love stories involve beating the odds. Well, in our story there was all kinds of odd and plenty of different kinds of beating. Even now, as I recall our story and watch her clapping for our kid with proud mama-bear enthusiasm, my heart inexplicably clenches, skipping a beat. Just like the first time I saw her. And the heart never lies.

BEST OF BOTH WORLDS
by Rhidian Brenig Jones

"WELL? WHAT D'YOU RECKON?"

Rhys's father had taken refuge behind the pages of the Telegraph and his mother was leaning straight-armed on the sink, looking out of the window. Cerys beamed at him.

The knot in his gut tightened. "Is Iain okay with it?"

Her smile lost some wattage. "Of course he is. Why wouldn't he be?"

"I don't know, I…" He shrugged. "I suppose, if that's what you want. It's your wedding."

"Thanks, Rhys. Thanks a bunch. Trust you to piss on my chips."

"Language, if you don't mind." The voice came with a snap of the newspaper, sharply chiding.

"Well, it's true."

His mother turned. "It's just come as a bit of a surprise to your brother, love. It's not what we expected, that's all. Don't you think morning dress would be—"

"Mum, don't be so bloody boring! I don't want morning dress."

Rhys ran a finger around the rim of his coffee cup. "Iain's people might see it as…well…kind of sucking up."

"Well, you'd know all about sucking, wouldn't you?"

"Cerys!" Fistfuls of paper crashing onto the kitchen table made them all jump.

His mother had the grace to redden and mutter an apology. She leaned across the table to touch Rhys's hand. "We're having kilts and that's the end of it, but I couldn't bear it if you weren't an usher. Mmm? Come on. There's a good boy."

***

Lounging on the sofa opposite him, Rhys's friends raised their brows to each other.

"Sure you don't want another lager?" When Rhys shook his head, Gareth lifted Steffan's legs onto his lap. "Cerys didn't mean to get at you, angel pie. She's bound to be stressed to buggery."

Rhys said nothing. His mind was still full of the excruciating silence that had followed his sister's sandbagging. If not exactly overjoyed, his parents seemed to have accepted his sexuality—as long as the unspeakable details of what gay sex might actually involve could be glossed over. He had been hugely embarrassed, more for their sake than his own, and he was still boiling.

"She was there for you when you came out, don't forget. Shut your nan up big time."

"I know."

Gareth stroked an arch and smiled briefly as his boyfriend's toes curled reflexively. "What's wrong with kilts, anyhow? Sounds okay to me."

"And me. All those hairy-arsed Scotties—"

"Hottie Scotties. Letting it all hang out."

Steffan grinned at Gareth. "Got to have the right bum for them, mind. Make those pleats swing."

"And everything else."

Rhys waited for their sniggers to subside. "Glad you find it so amusing."

"Ah, lighten up. It'll be cool."

"Yeah, if you're Scottish. We aren't. Welsh guys shouldn't be wearing kilts. No such thing till some genius invented them in the eighties."

"Don't see the problem. Scots, Irish, us. We're all supposed to be Celts, aren't we?"

Rhys rolled the empty lager can between his palms. "Different nations, different cultures. Kilts have got nothing to do with our culture. They're not authentic. Tell you what they are. Cultural appropriation."

"They're what?" Steffan asked, cracking open an eye.

"Explain later, babe. Anyhow, they're not. He's wrong." Prepared to argue the point, Gareth swung back to Rhys but broke off when he saw his friend's hand touching his ear: the unconscious, unmistakeable tell of his anxiety. Softening his tone he said, "It's like when you ducked out of Mike's thirtieth. You wouldn't go to that because it was fancy dress. You're scared that people'll be looking at you. But why wouldn't they, Rhys? You're bloody worth looking at, if you could only see it."

"Good night, that." Steffan wriggled his foot into Gareth's armpit. "Good laugh."

A muscle bunched in Rhys's jaw. "If you mean I don't want to look like a complete tool, you're right."

"You won't look like a tool, you'll look fabulous. A blond bombshell. Come on, Rhys, don't spoil things for Cerys."

"I'm not spoiling things. I've said I'll wear one, haven't I?"

"Yeah, but not with face like a fifty-pound fine." Gareth gurned a rictus grin. "Like this, see? Happy face. Happy face."

Rhys fell back against the sofa and stared at the ceiling. "Fuck."

***

His cousin and fellow usher blew into cupped hands. "If that twat doesn't stop fannying around any time soon, my balls'll be frozen to my kidneys."

The icy March wind that made the churchyard daffodils dance gusted under Rhys's kilt. Teeth clenched, he glanced to his left. The Scots at the other end of the line seemed unfazed by the polar chill; tough Northern lads or just no-nonsense guys swathed in thermal underwear while he froze in cotton Aussiebums?

"Right, gents." The stills photographer, snug in a down jacket, finally stopped fiddling with his camera. "Groom and best man, straight to me. Fathers, ushers, three-quarters profile. Close up a bit…that's the way. Big smiles on three, now. One, two…"

Interminable photographs finally taken, the line broke with laughter and stamping feet. Rhys held back as the others walked away, both to avoid the need for the small talk he dreaded and, more importantly, so that he could watch the tall figure strolling ahead of him: Callum, the second of his new brother-in-law's ushers, striking in the black and white tartan of clan MacFarlane.

His features were craggy, too rugged for conventional notions of male beauty, but his body, his magnetic masculinity, the sheer size of him, tugged at something in the pit of Rhys's stomach. He watched him bend to Laura, the prettiest of the bridesmaids, delicately fine-boned and flirtatious in vanilla silk. He took off his jacket and wrapped her in it, murmuring a few words that made her smile and duck her head. Callum would be gentle with her Rhys thought, watching them dispiritedly: conscious of the disparity in their sizes, he'd need to be. Gentle when his hands caressed her narrow hips, when he supported her, steadied her as she lowered herself, taking him in—

"Rhys!"

His father's shout jolted him back to the present.

"Come on, son, help get the cars sorted out."

As he passed through the lych gate, a different image rose, arrestingly vivid. Callum wouldn't need to be gentle with him.

***

"Please." Eight-year old Nancy hauled at his hand, noodle arms straining. "Pleeease."

Balanced on his shoes, he'd reluctantly shuffled her around the dance floor for fifteen hellish minutes under the amused eyes of the watching hordes. He touched her chest then flicked his finger to her chin as she looked down. "My feet are all squashed. Ask Daddy or Uncle Owen."

"I want to dance with you." Pouting, she pointed at his glass. "Can I have some?"

"Certainly not. It'd stunt your growth."

"What does that mean?"

"That it tastes nasty. Go on, clear off. I'll dance with you later."

"Promise?"

"Promise."

He watched her skip away to circle the dance floor, on the hunt for another victim. What if he, too, emerged from his bolthole in the corner and strode through the dancers to take a man by the hand? Lead him into the crush and hold him for a slow dance, swaying, hardly moving. It was what Gareth and Steffan would do if they were here, those ballsy queens not giving a rat's arse for any mutterings. He picked up his glass and downed the last of the vodka. Preposterous to imagine ever doing such a thing himself.

"Hey, brawd." Cerys gathered up the folds of her dress and sank onto a seat next to him. "You all right?"

"I'm good. You?"

Fingering the elaborate coils at her nape, she said, "My

hair's coming down a bit. You've scrubbed up pretty well, mind. Fair play. You look great in that kilt. All the boys do. I'm glad we went for the Glyndwr. The colours are so subtle."

Rhys studied the spread of cloth on his lap. Getting dressed that morning, he'd thought he might as well have had a giant arrow with KNOBHEAD! flashing in neon above his head but, truth be told, he hadn't felt as self-conscious as he'd feared. People seemed more interested in the kilt than the cripplingly shy man wearing it. It provided excellent camouflage.

Cerys said, "Owen isn't wearing pants. Nella cornered him and felt him up the back. Bare bum. Have you got drawers on?"

"God's sake, Cerys."

"Hey, nothing I haven't seen before. I used to bath you, remember, little brother."

He rolled his eyes. "Give it a rest."

"Okay. Listen. What I wanted to say, there's a bit of a problem. Some idiot messed up the bookings and they're one room short. Callum hasn't got one."

His stomach constricted. He'd only met the man a few short hours ago but just hearing the name acted on him like a cattle prod. "What about the Fleece? The King's? Have you tried them?"

"All full."

"The Marriott?"

"Do me a favour, Rhys, it's miles away. Anyway, he's been drinking. He couldn't drive."

It took a few seconds before it dawned on him where this might be leading. "Hang on, what are you saying?"

"You can put him up for a couple of nights, can't you? Your flat's only round the corner. Fall down twice, you're there."

He stared at her. "Put him up?"

"Why not? You've got a spare room. He can leave his car here and pick it up in the morning."

Rhys's flat was his private place. His home was his refuge, a blessed sanctuary, the one place where he was safe, where he could shut out the hurts of a hostile world. He tolerated his family there and a few trusted friends but the thought of those protective walls being breached by a stranger—a threatening stranger—terrified him. "Sorry, out of the question."

"Rhys, do you always have to be such a dick?"

"I mean it, Cerys. Not a chance."

"Hard luck. I've already told him it'll be okay."

"You've what?"

She half-rose and waved an arm. "Shut up. He's coming over."

Callum hadn't retrieved his jacket. Heavy shoulders spread from his waistcoat, curved with muscle. His tie was gone and a smudge of black hair was visible at the juncture of his collar bones, hinting at a pelt that would cover the broad planes of his chest and belly.

"…isn't it, Rhys?" Cerys kicked his ankle.

He had no idea what she'd said. He was aware only of the blood roaring in his ears and of dark eyes fixed on him.

He felt sick with anxiety but he managed a smile.

"If you're sure. I don't want to put you out." A rich baritone, a trace of huskiness roughening the accent. Educated Edinburgh: officer class.

"It's fine." Rhys cleared his throat. "You're welcome."

"Thanks. I appreciate it." Strong teeth flashed in a jaw blued by five o' clock shadow. "So, how about I get us a drink?"

***

Callum looked around with interest. His gaze settled on a group of flat screens, their snaking cables neatly tied and laid along the back of twin desks set at right angles to each other.

"That looks impressive," he said, putting down his bag.

Rhys realised that he was wringing white-knuckled hands. He loosened them and rubbed his forearm. "I…I'm a commercial artist. Illustrations for technical manuals and... I work from home."

"Yeah? I can't draw a straight line." He wandered across to the far wall, his head cocked as he considered a display of watercolour seascapes. "You do these? They're good."

"Don't know about that."

"They are. Really good. Are they local scenes?"

"Gower beaches. The big one there's Rhossili. It's been voted one of the best beaches in the world."

"Not surprised." He turned back and bent to study the painting more closely.

Free of those dark eyes, Rhys drank in the detail of the man: the perfectly cut line of hair above his collar; the solid waist bound by the chain of his sporran; the swell of his buttocks under the fall of the pleats. Despite his anxiety, the thought came of unbuckling Callum's kilt. The monochrome of the MacFarlane and the darker black and grey of the Glyndwr dropping together in soft woollen folds. Opening his legs for the slide of a warm palm on the inside of his thigh… "What do you do? Your work, I mean?"

Straightening, Callum said, "I'm a vet. Small animal practice, mainly, though I've been known to have my arm up the occasional cow's arse." Seeing Rhys's flicker of incomprehension, he smiled. "Checking for pregnancy."

"Oh. So you don't go up the, er…?"

"Vagina. No. Into the rectum and have a feel around."

God almighty. Vaginas, bovine or otherwise, being of minimal interest, Rhys said, "I'm sorry, I should have asked. Would you like a coffee or…?"

"Tell you the truth, I'm about ready for my bed just now. I was up at four for the flight."

"Sure. Of course, yes. Yes. I'll get the, er…bed made up. The bathroom's just there."

Callum picked up his case and followed Rhys into the hallway. Pausing, he said, "Thank you again. I owe you one."

His mind mostly on the forthcoming battle to wrangle

a quilt into a cover, Rhys nodded. "You're welcome."

"I've taken a few days off. Thought it would be a shame not to see a bit of Wales now I'm here. The Gower, further west to Pembrokeshire if there's time. I wouldn't mind taking a look at that beach."

"Rhossili."

"That's the one." He looked at his hand on the doorknob, then at Rhys. "Don't know how you're fixed, but would you fancy being my tour guide at all?"

A whole day? Another evening? Another night? Callum was easy-going—he certainly seemed relaxed as hell—but a straight Scottish vet and a gay Welsh artist? Sod all in common so sod all to talk about once the wedding had been dissected. Rhys felt rising panic. He was not good at the kind of small talk that came so effortlessly to others and the more stressed he became, the more he worried about boring people witless, the more he found himself stammering nonsense.

"Yes, I…" He made an effort to pull himself together. "Sure."

Callum's mouth quirked. "Great."

"Right, then. I'll, er, give you a shout in the morning."

"Not too early."

Rhys nodded. "No."

***

It was past three o'clock by the time Rhys parked the jeep on the cliff top. He'd spent a restless night, tossing and turning, slapping his hot pillow over to the cool side, aware of the head that lay only a foot away from his own at the other side of the wall. Intensely aware. Would Callum sleep naked? What did he look like, his powerful body sprawled in sleep? Rhys's imagining had brought his hand to his groin and, for a few indulgent moments, he'd surrendered to fantasy. He'd come quickly, silently, and release had finally brought sleepiness. Finally slipping into unconsciousness, he'd woken with a groan, unrefreshed at just before eleven.

If Callum had looked attractive in his kilt, he was mouth-watering when he ambled into the kitchen. Unshaven, hair wet from the shower, he'd dressed in soft old jeans—vintage 501s, Rhys suspected—and a navy V-neck sweater. Apparently unaffected by the rigours of the wedding party, he'd cheerfully demolished scrambled eggs and half a loaf of toast then, gesturing to Rhys's own eggs congealing unwanted on his plate, he'd polished them off, too. He'd been utterly at ease as he chatted about nothing in particular, and Rhys's anxiety had lessened as a result. Callum was sexy as hell, but, more, his warm and unforced friendliness soothed a shy man's fears.

Peering through the windscreen, Callum let out a whistle. "My God…"

The magnificence of Rhossili Bay lay beneath them, a vastness of golden sand curving three miles to the horizon. Pewter-grey under lowering cloud, the tide was high, whipped by the wind into turbulent white horses. To their right lay the cliffs of the downs and to the left the great jagged promontory of the Worm's Head reared from the sea.

"Doesn't look like a worm," Callum said.

"It's an old English word for dragon or sea serpent."

"Ah, right. Yeah, I see that." He unfastened his seat belt. "Shall we?"

Hunched against the buffeting wind, jackets billowing then flattening, they walked the path in silence. Rhys couldn't think of anything to say but Callum seemed content just to take in the scene and let the wind blow his hair into a wild black tangle. A couple of hardy souls in cagoules and hiking boots nodded as they passed, but apart from these they were alone. When they reached the tip of the headland, Rhys breathed a sigh of relief. He could talk about this without making a fool of himself. He pushed the hair out of his eyes. "You can walk the Worm when the tide's out but you've got to watch it. It's easy to get cut off."

"I bet."

"And see there?" He pointed back the way they'd come. "That place at the base of the cliff? It's an old rectory. Meant to be haunted. It's a holiday let now. Huge waiting list, by all accounts."

"Ghosties and ghoulies and long-leggedy beasties and things that go bump in the night…" He turned to Rhys with a lazy smile. "I like things that go bump in the night. And in the day, come to that. Given half a chance."

There was no mistaking his meaning. Rhys stared in a kind of paralysis. And as he stared, the smile faded from Callum's face to be replaced by an expression of clenched intent. The question was clear; his gaze locked on Rhys as he waited for the answer. But it seemed that Rhys, momentarily rendered even more speechless than usual by the revelation, had made him wait just that moment too long. The spell broke. Callum nodded to himself, as if acknowledging a faux pas. "Aye, right." He flipped his collar up around his ears. "Going to piss down in a minute. What d'you say we walk down to the beach then find somewhere to eat." He strode off and Rhys followed, inwardly cursing himself for his gutlessness. For being such a fucking, fucking idiot.

***

Replete after minted lamb shanks in a North Gower pub, Callum leaned back and stretched an arm along the back of the sofa. Exaggerating his accent, he said, "A braw wee place, right enough. Fine food."

"Yes, it's…well, I like it." The feelings of awkwardness that had faded over breakfast had come roaring back and once again, Rhys found it difficult to meet Callum's eyes.

"So tell me," Callum said, shifting a cushion at the small of his back, "did I offend you?"

At this, Rhys looked up. "Offend me?"

"When I came on to you."

A wash of colour heated Rhys's cheeks. "You didn't offend me."

"Thank Christ for that. Thought I'd read you wrong."

"You didn't."

"It's been known. So, there'll be no ladies in your life. But a significant other? A few significant others?"

Rhys surprised even himself at the bitterness of his laugh. "No."

"I'd have thought you'd have a queue forming outside, fighting to get in."

"Don't think so."

"D'you not? I would. Fight to get in." Amusement fanned fine creases at the corners of his eyes. "As it were."

The bubble of laughter in Callum's voice held no mockery, merely a hint of the pleasure he took in the mischievous flirtation. Gathering his courage, Rhys said, "I didn't think you were, er…Cerys didn't say." He wondered about this. She was usually quick off the mark, loving to elbow him in the ribs when a potential bed mate hove into view.

"It's no secret. So, am I of the homosexualist persuasion? To the bone. Maybe a wee bit too much of a chancer at times, mind you, but on the basis that God loves a tryer…"

Rhys smiled.

"A good-looking Welshman wearing the kilt? Now I find that particularly hard to resist."

The room became still, the air between them singing with promise.

Callum patted the sofa.

Heart thundering, Rhys held his gaze. Should he? Could he? God, it had been so long. Last year. Who had it been? The memory rose of the slim young Polish picture framer whose fractured English had proved little barrier to grasping Rhys's requirements in terms of mouldings, mountboards and glass, and none whatsoever when it came to a wild, grappling tussle which had ended with Rhys sprawled deliciously across his work bench, offcuts of pine digging into his belly. He took a decisive breath and crossed the floor to where Callum was waiting, and sat at his side.

Their first kiss was tentative, no more than an exploratory brush of lips on closed lips but it acted on Rhys like Callum had fastened his mouth on his cock. He drew away and drank in the sight of eyes fixed on him, even darker now and glittering with desire. He laid his palm on Callum's chest and Callum made to return the gesture, reaching towards Rhys's cheek.

"No! Don't!"

Callum jerked his hand away as if he'd been stung. "Jesus, what the fuck?"

"I'm sorry, I'm sorry." It was all he could say.

Shuffling away from him, Callum said, "I'm a big boy, Rhys. I can take getting the old heave-ho. You only had to say. No need for fucking melodrama."

"It's not that, it's not what you think. Oh, shit." Rhys hunched forward and stared blindly at the floor.

Callum spoke then with a horrible cold briskness. "I know well enough what I think. And just now, most of it is that it'll be a good idea if I get the hell out."

"No, please." He caught hold of Callum's wrist and tightened his grip. "Let me explain."

"Let go my arm."

Rhys did so. "Can I explain?"

Callum shrugged.

"It was my ear." He glanced at Callum, his heart sinking even further when he saw the hostility that had thinned the man's mouth. "I thought you were going to touch my ear."

"Your ear? What d'you mean? Why wouldn't I touch it?"

Rhys was no big drinker, but, by Christ, he needed one then. He got up and went into the kitchen. There was an unopened bottle of Finlandia in the cupboard, one he'd bought before finding out that Mike's idea of a birthday extravaganza didn't exactly accord with his own. He sloshed the vodka into two glasses and plinked in some ice. The bottle of tonic was half empty and probably flat. He poured it in anyway.

Callum's feathers still seemed ruffled, but at least he hadn't left. He took the proffered glass and sniffed dubiously before taking a swallow. "Well?"

"They called me Dumbo. Or Wingnut. Or FA, you know, after the FA Cup. Usually Dumbo, though." He saw himself so clearly, a little boy standing white-faced in a jeering ring of his peers. "They used to get me in the playground. They had this game. One would thump me in the back and when I turned, another one would see how many times he could flick my ears. It got worse. They stuck clothes pegs on a few times, and once, those metal clips you use for papers." He took a drink and wiped his mouth with the back of his hand. "Bulldog clips."

Callum's expression, if not entirely softened, had lost its granite immobility. "So what was it? Your ears stuck out?"

"More than stuck out. I think they were actually deformed. They stuck out at right angles to my head."

Considering Rhys, Callum said, "You had them fixed, obviously."

"Eventually. Took two goes. They were so bad they bent back after the first."

Callum poked an ice cube then licked a thoughtful finger. "Kids can be vicious little shits. There was an Italian girl when I was in High School. Graziella. Incredible acne. They called her Granola."

Rhys shook his head. He didn't mean to appear callous—he felt for the poor bitch—but he could do nothing for her and he needed Callum to understand, and he didn't, yet. "I was a shy kid anyway. I mean, agonisingly shy. I was probably born like that but the ears made me worse. Then, by the time they were fixed, I realised I was different in another way. Sometimes I think some crucial chip had failed in my motherboard, or maybe it wasn't there to begin with. The normality chip."

Callum frowned. He said sharply, "What bollocks are you saying? You don't feel normal? You're a hot, handsome, talented gay man. How's that not normal?"

As if he hadn't spoken, Rhys forced out the last drops of poison. "I was with this guy. We'd been going out for a few weeks. We were in bed one night and I told him all about my ears and the kids. He laughed. Fell about laughing. Couldn't stop. He thought the FA thing was the best because it could stand for Fucking Arsehole as well as FA Cup. He kept calling me it. Told some people. After that I kind of buried myself away. It's safer to be on my own."

"Jesus, Rhys."

"Yeah."

"What are you saying, you've never tried again? Tried to find someone who isn't a prick?"

"No."

"What d'you do for fun, for, well, for sex?"

"Pick-ups. Grindr."

"Fuck."

"When I thought you'd touch my ear I couldn't...I hate anyone touching them. Hate it. It reminds me. Stupid, I know, but I can't help it."

"Not stupid. Understandable. But unnecessary." Callum considered his drink, then downed it in one. "Don't normally drink this stuff."

Rhys sat up. "I'm sorry."

"No worries. It's not that bad."

"Not the vodka. For landing you with all this."

"D'you feel better for it?"

Something that had lodged in him for a long time had gone and its absence felt strange. Good, but strange.

"You seem better, that's for sure."

"Do I?"

"You've said more in the last twenty minutes than you have in the last twenty hours."

"Too much."

"Ach, not at all."

They weren't facing each other, each lost in his own thoughts. But even though there was a yard of space between them, Callum's warm understanding bridged it. Rhys closed his eyes and basked, allowing himself the luxury, if only for a brief time they had left. He had no doubt that Callum would leave soon; find somewhere to stay until his flight. There'd be plenty of hotel rooms near the airport.

"Rhys?"

"Yes?"

"I said God loves a tryer. Third time lucky, d'you think?"

When Rhys opened his eyes, there it was again, that lovely crooked smile. Slowly, he leaned towards it and slowly he lifted his face. Their kiss was as gentle as the first until Rhys rested his brow against Callum's and murmured against his mouth. "Thank you."

Careful to keep his fingers only to the curves of his jaw, Callum cupped Rhys's face. And this time, his mouth came down hard and open, his tongue delving, sliding and withdrawing to welcome Rhys's equally ferocious response.

"You really want to thank me?" He dropped one hand to the buttons of Rhys's shirt and flipped them open one by one. He slipped inside and found a nipple, and bared his teeth at the gasp of pleasure this brought from Rhys. "Then put the kilt on. Just the kilt. Nothing else.

"You like me in a kilt—oh, God, do that again…"

"I like you very much in a kilt. And I'm going to like taking it off you even more." Callum paused, as if struck by a thought. He trailed a finger from the cleft in Rhys's chin to the pulse pounding above his collar bone. Solemnly he said, "I don't want this to be a Grindr pick up. I think we might have something here."

"Yes."

"Yes indeed. Have you ever been to Scotland?"

Surprised, Rhys said, "The farthest north I've been is Durham."

"Fancy visiting some time?"

Rhys blushed, this time with pleasure. He nodded fervently.

"Good. We'll work something out. But for now…" Pushing Rhys's shirt off his shoulders he smiled, and it was not the sudden coolness that made Rhys shudder but the caressing touch between his thighs. "I really, really, really want to see a hunky Welshman in his kilt.

A PAINTING OF LOVEBIRDS AGAINST A FRACTURED BACKGROUND

by Shelley Ross-Winter

MORE THAN TEN YEARS HAD PASSED since we last saw each other.

I'd moved on, worked hard, got a finance job in the city and rented myself a flat twenty minutes away on the tube. You know, sensible, adult things. Sure, I still thought of myself as an artist. I still held tight to that little bit of hope. But I also had to earn a living. Dreams were exciting, but they didn't put food on the table.

To tell you the truth, I don't think I ever expected to see him again, let alone there and then. The monotony of existence had turned me into just another zombie: earphones blasting, screeching heavy metal direct to my brain, head hanging loose, shuffling with the crowd as it carried me into the tube station, knowing there would be too many people for the first train and not caring.

I just planned to push my way onto the second.

The tap on my shoulder almost passed me by. Then it came again, more insistently this time. I reluctantly turned, grabbing the earbud out of my ear and preparing to say "no thanks, mate" or "that way" or whatever response would get me away quicker.

When I saw him, I swear my heart stopped.

"Hey, Picasso."

What was he even doing here? Shouldn't he be in Japan or China or wherever it was that Sewer Rat had sold all their records? "Alex," I said, in the same tone I'd use for ordering train tickets from an automated phone line.

"You look good, Nate. How are you?"

I looked good? Was he mocking me? It had been more than a decade and he hadn't aged a day. Same easy smile, same blonde hair loose down to his shoulders, same rough beard from not bothering to shave for a couple of days. He looked lost inside a crumpled, baggy Duran Duran T-shirt that looked like it hadn't seen an iron since the 80s ... I glanced down, already knowing what I'd see.

The wind plastered the kilt to his legs like a second skin, shrink-wrapping his thighs in grey tartan.

Same old Alex. The world might have moved on, but he refused to come along for the ride.

"It's good to see you." I nodded and tried to force a smile. "I need to catch the next train."

"You won't catch this one. There'll be another in ten seconds."

"Five minutes." I corrected, as if I didn't recognise hyperbole when I heard it.

"Miss it." He lightly grabbed my arm as I tried to pull away. There was no force to it. I could have slipped from his grip. "Have dinner with me."

"I can't. I'm having dinner with a friend." The lie came easily, but then I always was good at that.

A moment of doubt passed over his face and I could tell he believed me. "Tomorrow then."

"No."

I gulped back the dryness in my mouth, counting the moments. All the assertiveness courses in the world couldn't make that single word any less terrifying. My stomach churned.

"Wait, take this." He shoved a piece of card into my hand, and I pretended not to see the tears brimming in his eyes. "It was good to see you, Nate."

I nodded and left him without another word.

**

I was an art undergrad when I first met Alex.

At that time, he was just another wannabe, drifting along on temp jobs and weed, playing guitar and singing to the middle-aged stoners in the only dives that still hired punk rock bands. Sewer Rat's bass player, a green-and-pink-haired girl who called herself Bella Donna, was going out with my best friend, Aleesha. She dragged me along to one of her girlfriend's gigs and it was there that I first saw him.

It was instant infatuation.

I have no illusions about that initial attraction. He was tall, lean, sculpted and exotic. Eyeliner and plucked eyebrows, lipstick and lace gloves, all somehow enhancing his masculinity rather than belying it. He wore work boots with no laces that clattered and clomped and nearly fell off his feet while he commanded the stage, kilt billowing and flapping as he turned and screamed and bellowed and posed. He was a showman, a peacock, and I was smitten. When I met him I could hardly speak. He saw my blushes and did everything in his power to keep them coming.

We got along so well, I completely lost track of the time.

Maybe Aleesha knew I'd fall for him. She certainly did nothing to discourage it. I already had a boyfriend, but she had never been keen on Stephan. On the way home she told me Alex was bi, that he'd had a couple of girlfriends and a short fling with a man, that he and Bella had formed the band one night after a drug-fuelled shag in her dad's garden shed.

"Bella's bi?" I asked.

Aleesha shook her head and laughed. "More lesbian than a hot girl in a Subaru. She was just stoned and horny. It was the worst sex of her life, apparently. But don't let that put you off."

She winked and I blushed and tried to hide the smile that played on my lips.

***

"You'll never guess who I bumped into today."

I held the phone to my ear as I carried the plate of pasta and vegetables through to the living room in my small apartment. Most of the room was filled with my artwork, much of it unfinished. A few pieces adorned the walls, others were stacked behind the sofa.

I didn't wait for Aleesha's response.

"Alex Rindal."

"No way, really?" She barely missed a beat before adding, "Was Bella with him?"

"Not that I saw. Why? Are you still interested?"

"I don't know. Maybe. I miss her. How's Alex?"

"Seems okay." I shoved a forkful of food into my mouth, then spoke around it. "Same old Alex, really. Great hair, mascara, kilt. We didn't talk for long."

"Okay ..."

"What?"

"Nothing! Just that you seem to be trying too hard to sound disinterested. And you two were cute together."

"We never were together, Leesh. He was just there at a difficult time, that's all."

"And if he hadn't left to go on tour you would have boned until you both died of exhaustion."

I rolled my eyes and let the silence speak for itself.

"Anyway, you must have said something to each other."

"He asked me to dinner."

She laughed. "He loves you! He loves you!"

"He doesn't. Anyway, I said no." I shifted awkwardly on the sofa, the thought of him making me uncomfortable. "I don't need to be reminded of all that."

"Do I remind you of it?"

"No, but that's different. We were friends before."

"And he was a friend to you when you needed one. Plus, he's hot. I've seen recent pictures on the Sewer Rat website. You really should check it out."

"I literally saw him in person today. And I suppose there are pictures of Bella on there as well, right?"

"Maybe. If there were photos of her half naked and giving sexy eyes I really didn't notice."

I snorted a laugh. "He gave me a card. It's got his number on it."

"And you want me to persuade you to call it, huh?"

"No ..."

"You know what I think, Nate. Call him, have dinner with him, pump him for Bella's phone number. And yes, that was subtle innuendo."

"You wish it was subtle. If you want her number so bad, you call him."

"I don't have his number."

"I'll give it to you."

"Ugh." She sighed in exasperation. "Hang up on me. Call Alex. Just have dinner with him, Nate, you owe him that. See how things go. Maybe you walk away knowing that you've closed that chapter. But maybe you find that actually it's not so bad seeing him again."

"Maybe—"

"I'm hanging up."

I laughed self-consciously, but the line went dead.

Perhaps she was right. Perhaps I did owe Alex at least a conversation. I shoved another forkful of food into my mouth and thought as I chewed, staring at the card discarded on the table beside my laptop. I could just call him, of course, there'd be no harm in that. Or text. Instead, I flipped open my laptop and waited for it to come out of sleep mode.

As I finished off the last of the food, I logged onto eBay and clicked on my account, then blinked.

A sale.

"Oh my God."

Three hundred and fifty pounds for one of my most recent paintings: lovebirds cuddling into each other against a background of impressionist glass shards. They'd paid the buy it now price. There wasn't even a single bid before that.

It was more than seven times my best sale to date.

"Yes!" I did a little fist pump as I grinned. "Yes, yes! Oh my ..." I wriggled in the seat, my mind racing with possibilities. The idea of quitting my job and working full time as an artist floated into my head. Which of course was ridiculous after only one sale. But still, it was exciting. "This is big time," I muttered to myself as I reached for the card with Alex's number and started typing into my phone.

Me: Hey, it's me Nate. I sold a painting today!

I clicked send without a second thought, then sent a similar message to Aleesha. I would have sent a mass email to the whole world if I could. The thought that my work was actually good enough for someone to want to pay money for it—real money, too, the kind that actually meant something—was intoxicating. Would I actually be able to get any more work done tonight?

My phone beeped and I picked it up.

Aleesha: Wow, that's great, for how much?

I grinned as I started typing the message, then before I could send it, the text from Alex came through.

Alex: Fantastic! So, dinner is on you?

My heart skipped a beat. How the hell did he manage to do this to me? How did he make me feel this way after a single chance encounter? My fingers tingled as I hovered over his message. Dinner. We could just go to dinner. I mean, I knew this little place that wasn't too far away, intimate and quiet. The owners knew me.

Alex: Let me take you out to celebrate, please? No pressure, just old friends catching up.

Me: I already ate.

A second went by before the phone beeped again.

Alex: Tomorrow then. 8pm. And I was joking about you paying. It's my treat. What do you say?

I took a deep breath, then started typing before I could talk myself out of it.

Me: Sure, OK. Where shall we meet?

Alex: Do you remember The Silver Finger?

I snorted a laugh and shook my head, crossing one leg over the other as I relaxed back into my seat. He literally hadn't changed. How could so many years have passed him by without affecting him the way they had the rest of us? Everyone else I had known that long had grown cynical or serious, life had worn them down. Even

Aleesha had got involved in more organised activism rather than just turning up for demonstrations whenever she heard about them.

Alex was just, well, Alex. Nothing had changed for him. Despite fairly major success for his band in other parts of the world, he could come back here and still be the twenty-four-year-old I fell in love with.

I felt my heart clutch. Fell in love with? Was that true or was it just nostalgia? We were friends. Almost intimate, but never quite. It just wasn't the right time for a relationship when I finally got away from Stephan's abuse. Alex had to go away on tour and I never tried to contact him ... hardly the actions of someone that was in love, right?

Aleesha: Answer me! How much?!?!

Me: £350. Alex has invited me to The Silver Finger tomorrow night.

The phone started ringing, her name and photo filling the screen. I hesitated for a moment before answering.

"I haven't said I'm going yet," I lied. I could always get out of it.

"But you will, Nate. Come on, that's pretty romantic that he remembered where he first met you."

"Maybe. I don't even know if I would fit in there anymore. I'm not sure I did back then."

She laughed, then sighed when I didn't respond. "You really don't know who owns The Silver Finger now? God, Nate, you live in a world of your own. Eliot James? No? Australian guy, known for his barbecued food?"

"I think I might have heard of him ..." I trailed off. The name didn't mean a thing to me.

"Ugh. You're such a liar. The place has a big fire pit right out in the open and you can watch the food being cooked in front of you. It's bloody expensive."

"Hold on, Alex just sent a text."

Alex: Or somewhere else if you'd prefer?

"Go to dinner with him, Nate. Fantastic news about the painting. Congratulations. Tell me how things go with Alex."

"I love you."

"Just tell him you'll go."

"Speak to you tomorrow?"

"If you're not too busy ..." She giggled. "I'll want details! Bye!"

She clicked off and I rolled my head on my neck, then brought up Alex's text and typed out a reply.

Me: Sorry, I had a call. I remember it. I'll meet you there.

Alex: Fantastic! 8pm. See you there.

I let my eyes close as I thought about him, trying to work out my own feelings. It was just dinner, I told myself, but I knew that was a lie. Nothing between me and Alex was ever just anything. Right from the start, there was a spark. As I let the images come, I couldn't stop myself thinking about the first time we were alone...

***

Aleesha had barely waited a week before bringing Alex to visit me, making some lame excuse to leave us there alone while she went off into town.

"These are amazing," Alex said, rifling through my sketches. "Really amazing."

"Thanks." I pulled one of my boyfriend's folders from the cabinet and laid it open. "Stephan's the real artist though."

Alex nodded. "He's good. But you're a regular Picasso." His voice was matter-of-fact, as if it was obvious. "Are these yours too?"

He wandered over to the two large canvases. Studies of broken pottery and dead roses in thick acrylic paint. I was experimenting with my style at the time, trying different mediums and different representations. The pottery looked impressionistic, the flowers more cubist. "Yes," I muttered, coming up behind him. "Just practice pieces."

"Do you ever do people?"

I shrugged. "I have done. In class."

"Nudes?"

My throat felt dry. I coughed nervously. "Female nudes."

"I'd pose for you. If you wanted to do a male, I mean."

He turned and met my eyes, and I didn't have a response. Was he teasing? Trying to get me to laugh? I stood there gawping.

"I think all bodies are beautiful, don't you?"

I nodded. "Maybe you could speak to the university. I think they pay their—"

"I wouldn't want any money." He turned and

sauntered out in front of the canvases, where the pots and flowers lay strewn. "Here?"

"What?" My mind raced. Was he serious? "I'm not ... I haven't got a canvas prepared." I almost died with embarrassment at my own words. "We should find out where Aleesha is."

"She's fine," he said, gripping the hem of his Cyndi Lauper T-shirt and dragging it up over a slim, defined belly, devoid of hair. Half of me wanted to flee, the other half was working out the light and shadow of ribs, light pectorals, tiny hard nipples. "Shall I put my clothes here?"

I nodded as he draped the shirt over a stool and started kicking off his boots.

"Yes, wherever ..." This couldn't happen. Any artwork I did right now would be a mess. "You can change in the bedroom if you want," I said, taking a step back and reaching out to feel for my pencil on the table. "There's a robe you could—"

"I'm good," he said, turning and meeting my eyes as he leaned down to remove his mismatched socks. He held my gaze, and I could hardly breathe. "I can't wait to see your work." He started to unbuckle his kilt, sliding the leather strap through the loop in the fabric and holding on as it went loose.

My blood shot low, my balls tightening as I started to get hard. I tried to shift into a more comfortable position, something that would hide my obvious arousal, but as I thought about it I only grew harder. I couldn't take my eyes off him, watching as he dragged the wraparound tartan across his body, then paused.

"Do you want to help?"

"I don't ..." I shook my head. "No. We should stop."

"I don't want to stop," he said. "And nor do you."

"I can't. Alex, please."

He shrugged and pulled the kilt open, turning to drop it on top of the discarded T-shirt. A pair of black briefs rode up one buttock and barely covered his growing bulge.

"No. Stop," I whispered, wanting him to ignore me.

He took the waistband of his briefs between his thumb and forefinger, then paused.

"If you want me to stop, I'll stop."

My lips moved, the blood drained from my face. "I ..." There was no way to finish the thought, no way to wrangle my brain into any kind of coherence.

"I want to kiss you, Nate." His voice was breathy, a little scared. "I want to fuck you."

The words made my skin tingle. If I expected him to take the decision away from me, I was disappointed. He remained motionless. He'd told me what he wanted, now it was up to me.

My heart thundered. "I want to—"

I heard the click of Stephan's key in the door and every bone in my body froze. Stepping back, I shook my head.

"He can't find you here. Not like this. Please!"

"Okay." Alex nodded, not questioning my reasons. "Is there another way out?"

"The back door. Through there." I pointed towards the kitchen. "Hurry, please!"

"Don't panic." He bundled his discarded clothes into his arms and slid his feet into the boots.

Without bothering to get dressed, he fled from the room, and Stephan never knew a thing.

*****

"My Picasso." Alex grinned as he stood to greet me at the table. Part of me railed against the nickname, but another part felt light on my feet, both over the reminder of my recent success and the idea that I was his.

"It's one sale," I said, holding my hand out to shake. Instead, he grabbed me around the shoulders and pulled me in for a hug.

"One of many, I'm sure."

I shrugged as he released me and stepped back. "I've sold a few in the past, never for this much."

He grinned and sat down, shifting his seat around the table, closer to the one that had been left for me. As I sat, he folded one leg over the other, adjusting his trademark kilt over his knees.

"I'm so glad you agreed to come." He held his hands up. "Just as friends, of course."

"Well, let's see how things go." My heart almost broke despite myself. It stung to hear him close off the possibility of more, and that shocked me. Did I want this to go further? "It's been a long time."

"Too long." A smile played on his lips, a light behind his eyes that made me feel giddy. What was he thinking? What was he imagining?

What was he hoping for?

We ordered food and Alex flirted openly with me. It felt awkward at first, but then, much to my own surprise, I started to relax into his company and the safety that came with knowing someone so well. He wasn't pushy or assuming, there was no attempt to wow me with his successes. But it was clear he would have liked to pick up where we left off.

I ate skewers of barbecued tomatoes, courgettes and goats' cheese, while Alex had smoked and seasoned tempeh with a side salad. I'd been vegetarian since I left home, but Alex had been a vegan when I met him. We chatted about the environment, how governments needed to take responsibility, and he told me about a walk he did between two gigs a hundred miles apart to raise awareness and money for environmental charities. Apparently, it was all on his website; I had to admit that I hadn't looked.

"I've kept up with your artwork," he said with a grin. "Your website looks professional."

I laughed. "I made it myself. It's just WordPress."

He nodded. "I never was any good at that stuff. We have a web designer that works with us, otherwise we wouldn't have anything."

"Is the band doing well? I never hear anything. Aleesha despairs of me."

"How is she?"

"She's good. She'd like Bella's phone number." I looked down at my empty plate, embarrassed, and then reached for my wine glass.

Alex chuckled. "Bella asks about her, too. Those two should have never split up."

I met his eyes and felt my breath quicken. There was a subtext in his words. Those two. We two.

"Well, Sewer Rat is doing as well as it's ever done really. No sign of breaking into the British or American charts any time soon, or even the Australian ones for that matter, but we've got our own fans in Asia and Eastern Europe and I'm happy to be out of the limelight over here." He bit the end of his tongue between his lips, as if considering whether to say the next words, but then ploughed ahead. "I'm not struggling, Nate. I have money, and more time for a ... personal life."

I nodded but hesitated, then forced myself to speak. "Is this ..." I pointed between the two of us. "... going somewhere?"

"I want it to."

We stared into each other's eyes for what felt like an age, and my heart rate thundered. "Me too," I said, finally.

It felt like we were the only two people in the world.

***

I offered to pay half towards the meal, but Alex wouldn't let me. He leaned over the table as I reached for my wallet and grabbed my hand, pulling it between both of his and staring into my eyes as he shook his head.

"My treat. I said so. Besides, you may have sold one

painting but you're not Antony Gormley yet."

I smirked. "He's a sculptor. I'm not trying to be him."

Alex shrugged. "Whatever. Show-off. When you've sold a few more pieces I'll let you pay for dinner." He stood and strode away to the desk.

I watched him go, wondering where things were heading and chastising myself for the fear I'd felt about this meeting. Alex wasn't Stephan, and he didn't remind me of Stephan in any way. The truth was, in the years since we last saw each other, I hadn't really had a boyfriend at all, certainly nothing serious. And that was kind of okay, too. I had to give myself as much time as I needed. But things were different now, and for the first time in a long time I could see a future. A romantic future with Alex. And possibly one that included making an income—maybe only a part-time income, but an income nonetheless—from my art work.

My phone buzzed in my pocket and I grabbed it, unlocking it in the hope that it was Aleesha and I could gush about how the evening was going, but it was just an email from PayPal letting me know that the funds for the painting had cleared into my bank account. A little part of me did a jump for joy as I looked at the amount. Maybe not a lot per hour of work, but a decent amount for an unknown painter.

But it reminded me that I still needed to send the painting. I opened the email from eBay to check on the buyer's name and address and set myself a reminder. The address was in London, a flat over in Camden. I smiled to myself. It was a trendy area with a good music scene, the sort of area Alex and I would have loved to live.

Perhaps the sort of area we would live together one day?

I know. Stupid to let my mind run away with me. But it was a happy fantasy. And it was possible. Who knew where things would lead between us?

The buyer, Dilan Laxer, had put the sale through a corporate credit card, so no doubt an executive of some kind. SR Music Productions Ltd. Very intriguing. I wondered if Alex knew him.

Then it clicked. I don't know why I didn't see it until now, but it was right there. I counted the letters in the names and fitted them together, and knew it couldn't just be a coincidence.

The flat in Camden, which fitted so perfectly, the music production company with the initials SR, the fact that Alex hadn't asked once how much the painting sold for. I mean, it could have been a tenner or a million pounds as far as he knew. Except he did know, didn't he?

Because Dilan Laxer was an anagram of Alex Rindal.

I looked over at Alex, standing there paying for the meal on his credit card. Was it a corporate card for SR Music Productions Ltd? It had to be Sewer Rat's production company. I was such an idiot. The heat rose to my face as I thought about how much of a fool I must look to him. Was he laughing at me? Of course he wouldn't let me pay for the meal. Sewer Rat must be bringing in so much from their Asian customers that it was a drop in the ocean. Certainly a fair amount for ... oh, no. No, no, no.

That was it, wasn't it? I was just a distraction while he was back in the country.

As the dominoes fell, I felt my stomach start to churn. I was going to throw up. He'd handed me some money for a painting, treated me to dinner, of course he was expecting something in return.

I stood, grabbing my jacket off the back of the chair and almost knocked another diner off his as I fled the room. I felt like everyone's eyes were burning a hole in my back, like they all knew exactly what had happened and it had all been some big setup.

Alex shouted after me, asking what was wrong, but I ignored him. I ran out into the night, pulling my coat around my shoulders against the chill that I could have sworn wasn't there earlier. It was a summer's evening, it should be warm and comfortable, but I felt frozen. There was a tube station just down the road from the restaurant and I headed straight for it.

***

It was four months after Alex almost modelled nude for me in the house I shared with Stephan when, late one Friday evening, he, Bella and Aleesha helped me to flee. With Sewer Rat's Ford Transit parked on the double-yellows out the front, the four of us worked hastily to load my belongings into the back before Stephan was due home. I didn't have a lot, to be honest, just clothes, canvases, art materials and a tall mirror given to me by my nan when she'd passed away. But I was glad of the help because, despite knowing it was the right thing to do, I needed the moral support.

Until I met Alex, Stephan had been everything to me. I was so infatuated with him that I didn't even see how things really were between us. He was a fellow art student, but from a completely different world. His parents were rich enough to rent him a house with space for a studio and to furnish him with an allowance that kept us both comfortable. Stephan had wooed me with expensive meals and gifts, had encouraged me to give up my part-time job in Sainsbury's to pursue my art full time. He was never ashamed of me, the way my previous boyfriend had been, he wanted to display me, he wanted to be seen with me. It was romantic and safe.

At first.

Perhaps I should have known sooner. Perhaps I should have seen the signs when he called my manager at the supermarket and handed the phone to me, ordering me to tell him I quit. Perhaps I should have gotten out when he made the snide comments about my art or when he sulked every time I went out with my friends. But I didn't. All I saw was a man in love, a man who I loved deeply and completely. When he hit me the first time I was so shocked I didn't even say anything. I just hid the bruise beneath a thick jumper and went on as normal, telling myself that it didn't mean anything. The next time I convinced myself it was my own fault, I'd been late getting home and forgot to call. He was worried about me. The time after that I just accepted it as a part of who we were, telling myself that it was a sign of how passionately he felt about me.

Aleesha, of course, knew nothing about the violence until a week before she helped me get out. She knew about the controlling aspects. How could she not? But when she'd told me the relationship was unhealthy I'd thrown it back in her face. It's a testament to how good a friend she was that she had brushed that off without a word. She'd told me she wouldn't do anything, that she couldn't force me to leave him, but that Stephan wasn't right for me. As soon as I showed her the bruises, tearfully admitting that I was scared of him, she'd said I could stay with her, and that's when we'd formed the plan to get me out.

Once all my stuff was loaded into the van, Alex came back inside with me to make one last check of the house. To tell you the truth, I knew I hadn't left anything behind, but a part of me wanted to take one last look at the place I'd called home for the last year and a half.

"You'll get another place," Alex told me as he watched me wander around the studio. "Somewhere you'll be safer."

"Yeah," I said, trying to sound confident but failing. I wasn't from the kind of family that expected to have money or an easy life. My parents had been disapproving when I chose an art degree. My dad had given me a talk about how it would put employers off. At the time, I didn't care, but now ...

"I, um ... I like you, Nate."

I turned to find Alex staring at me, arms folded across his chest. There was a forced half smile on his face and it was the first time I'd ever seen him vulnerable like that. I opened my mouth, but wasn't sure what to say.

"Sorry, probably bad timing. I'm an idiot."

I shook my head. "No. The timing is perfect, it's what I need to hear. I like you too."

He visibly relaxed. "Thank God for that." His laugh was awkward. "I was hoping that we could maybe, you know, get a bite to eat sometime or something?"

"That would be nice. Just give me a little time to get my head straight?"

He nodded. "Take as long as you need." The silence that followed felt strained.

"I've got something for you." I hadn't intended to give it to him, but I didn't want things to be awkward. "In the van. Come on."

Outside I dug through the canvases and handed him the smallest one there. It wasn't very good, I'd been working from memory, but it still made me blush to let him see it.

The grin on Alex's face was mischievous. "Is that how you imagined it? Or have you been spying on me?"

I snorted a laugh. "Who said it's you?"

"I love it, Picasso. Thank you."

Aleesha's voice echoed from the front seats. "What are you two up to back there? We need to get going."

It felt like the beginning of something special, but two

weeks later Sewer Rat's self-promoted record started to make some real tremors in the underground scene in Tokyo and Phnom Penh, and some record producer signed them up for an Asian tour. Alex asked me to go with them, told me that he'd buy me a plane ticket home any time I wanted, but I turned him down. I told him I would call and we could carry on getting to know each other when he got back.

It was the last time I would see him until we met on that underground platform.

***

"Slow down; what's happened?" Aleesha's voice on the other end of the line was a comfort, a familiarity that I needed, and I could feel my heart rate slowing. I sat on a bench, tears streaming down my face, and I should have been embarrassed, but I wasn't. Let the other people waiting on the platform stare. I didn't care.

There was a hitch in my voice as I spoke. "It was him. That painting I sold. Fuck, I'm such an idiot. Why did I let myself believe it?"

"What was him?"

"The painting. The buyer. It was Alex." I wiped a hand down my face and sniffed. "It was just Alex. Just a way to get me to go to dinner."

"He told you that?"

I shook my head, even though she couldn't see me. "He didn't have to. SR Music Productions Limited. SR. Sewer Rat."

"That's a bit of a—"

"The buyer's name was Dilan Laxer, Leesh."

"I..." She made a sighing noise. "I don't know who that is. Is he—"

"He is Alex. Alex Rindal is Dilan Laxer. One's an anagram of the other."

"Oh, shit."

I took a deep breath, starting to calm down as I talked it through. "Yeah, exactly."

"And what did he have to say for himself?"

"I have no idea. I ran out. I couldn't face him. He must have thought it was a right laugh, me being so proud of the sale when the whole time it was just him messing with me."

"That doesn't sound like Alex though."

"Yes it does. It sounds like every man I've ever been involved with." I was starting to raise my voice. People were staring. "He's no different."

There was a pause on the other end of the line. "I'm not saying he's not a class A asshole for doing that, but I doubt he did it to hurt you, Nate."

"Why not though, Leesh? It's the sort of thing Stephan would have done, just to show me that his art was so much better because he had made enough money to be able to buy mine. Why not Alex? His band is obviously doing well, what with a flat in Camden and fancy restaurants and—"

"He's not Stephan," she cut me off.

"He might as well be." I took a deep breath and allowed silence to fill the space. I didn't want to alienate my best friend. "Anyway, I'm going to refund him the money."

The next voice came from beside me. "Please don't do that, Nate."

I glanced up, then turned away as I said, "What are you doing here?"

"I came to find you."

"I'm fine. Leave me alone."

"Is that Alex?" Aleesha sounded irritated on my behalf. If I put her on speaker, she'd probably give him a piece of her mind.

"Nate, please." Alex sighed. "Can I sit down?"

I shrugged. "It's a free country, I guess. My train will be here in a minute anyway."

"Look, I'm guessing you know that I bought the painting." I felt him take the seat on the bench beside me. "I should have told you that it was me. I'm sorry."

I spoke into my phone. "Aleesha, I'm going to have to call you back in a minute, I need to catch this train."

"Let me speak to him."

I ended the call, cutting her off.

"It's fine. I'm an idiot. You can go home and laugh about it. Please, leave me alone."

Alex tried to put his hand on my shoulder, but I shrugged away. "Nate, don't be like that. Nobody's laughing at you, least of all me."

"I don't need another controlling boyfriend." My lip quivered as I said the words, trying not to look at him. "I had enough of that with Stephan. I thought you were different."

"I am different. I'm not trying to control you."

"Really? You bought a painting just to get me to go to dinner with you. Possibly you thought I might sleep with you as well." I shrugged. "That's pretty controlling, Alex."

"Is that what you think ... no. No. Nate, you're wrong."

I snorted a breath. "And now you're trying to gaslight me. Nice. You could just admit it and apologise. I'd respect you more. I'm still not going to sleep with you though."

"I am sorry, Nate. But I didn't do it to control you. I'm not trying to get you into bed and I'm not laughing at you either. Please, let me explain."

"Say whatever you like. My train is going to be here in about thirty seconds, and if you follow me on I'll call the police."

"I can't even imagine how much Stephan hurt you, but I'm not him. I should have told you that it was me who bought the painting, and yes, a part of me was over the moon when I got the text from you so excited about it. And maybe I hoped it would get you to go to dinner, but only because you were in a better mood. I'm an asshole for not being upfront with you."

He moved closer on the bench and I didn't try to move out of the way. But a part of me wanted to cry. Everything that I'd hoped for just half an hour ago was now lying broken in pieces on the floor, and I didn't know if I would ever get it back.

"... please stand back from the platform edge ..." The automatic announcement droned on.

I stood as people gathered on the platform, and Alex followed me into the crowd, raising his voice to be heard as if he didn't care who else was there. Some people were looking at him like they recognised him. Maybe they did.

"I didn't buy the painting for myself, Nate. I have a friend who's an art dealer. I showed her some of your work and she loved it, she said that if I had any she'd buy it from me. Getting your work into her gallery is the kind of thing that can launch a career. Her buyers are the movers and shakers."

I turned his way and rolled my eyes, trying to figure out just how stupid he thought I was. "And this art dealer friend of yours couldn't buy any of my work herself, I suppose. She absolutely had to have you buy it for her."

He opened his mouth to start to speak, then went red in the face. The train pulled into the station and people moved forward before it had even come to a stop. Alex's next words were hesitant. "Andrea's a dealer, she's all business. She would have paid you the market value. I mean, the current market value. You would have got ten pounds, maybe fifteen. And she would have sold it for hundreds. I couldn't let that happen."

I paused, half seething, half swooning.

It was kind of sweet, even if it was misguided. "That's still kind of an asshole thing to do."

He nodded. "I know. The only painting I already had of yours was the one you gave me and I wasn't going to sell that. So I had to buy another."

The train doors slid open and people moved forward, pushing to get on board as others were pushing to leave.

I blinked away tears. "You kept it?" The words spilled from my mouth before I could stop them. I felt the blush rise to my face at the thought of the painting, what it meant to me at the time, how much emotion I'd poured into it.

When I saw Alex turn a deep crimson, any resolve I had to leave him fled.

"I took it with me when I went on tour. I hoped you'd call me, Nate; you never did."

The doors to the train swooshed closed. I stayed where I was. There were tears in the corners of Alex's eyes and I moved on instinct, reaching out and putting my arms around his shoulders. There was a hitch to his breathing, a sob waiting to release, and I wanted to make the pain go away.

"Sorry," I muttered, holding him close. "I was hurt and I lashed out."

"I'm sorry, too."

I nodded against his shoulder. "Apology accepted." I took a deep breath. "Don't ever do anything like that again."

Alex laughed and shook his head, looking down at his feet.

"Please will you buy me dessert?"

He spluttered on his own tears and nodded. "The least I can do, Picasso."

"So ..." I said, pulling away and taking his hand in mine. "Pretty narcissistic to take a painting of yourself on tour."

He squeezed my hand as we started walking towards the station entrance.

"You never admitted it was me."

BRING ON THE HEAT
by Meyari McFarland

DEVON STOPPED INSIDE THE MOVING VAN, sweat dripping down his nose, neck, forehead, back, and knees. Everywhere... He dragged the hem of his Rammstein T-shirt up and mopped his face with it, even though it was soaked through already. Those assholes should be out here helping with the last few boxes like they'd promised.

Given the heat, though, it was probably better that they weren't. None of the guys were all that good at dealing with this high temperature, so they all stripped down at a moment's notice. Which meant Devon was doomed, especially if certain people, An especially, took their shirts off.

He'd lived in the Puget Sound for twenty-some years now, having come for college and then never left, but damn, this was one of the hottest days he'd experienced. Their little farm outside Granite Falls, Washington was still green and lush. Enough rain fell throughout the year to keep it green well into the middle of August. But it felt dusty today instead of right on the verge of the plants taking over the world.

An had taken off his shirt barely five minutes into moving boxes. In response, Devon had tripped on his own feet and nearly face-planted in a box of books. Nothing could mess with his coordination as fast as An stripped to the waist. Devon was going to spend the next several years running into walls every time An showed the littlest bit of skin.

The only thing that saved Devon from smashing the box and his face was Noy catching him before he lost his balance entirely. Between An's lean torso and wiry arms, Noy's thighs under his short-shorts, Placide's snark and smirking and Hanne ordering Devon around, it was a miracle that Devon hadn't broken every single thing he'd carried today. Every bit of his embarrassment and suppressed attraction was worth it for their farm though.

Twenty acres of land, half forested with huge old cedars too big for Devon to have his fingers meet if he hugged them. The undergrowth, what little there was, full of ferns and moss as thick as a shag carpet. He'd thought, when they toured the land together, that the moss was the inspiration for shag carpets. Miniature forest right there under the forest canopy.

This half, their house's half, was farmland that'd been left to run wild after the last owner died and his kids chose not to come to take care of the place. Wild chickens clucked off by the big barn that had one corner collapsing into rot. The kitchen garden looked like solid grass to

Devon but An swore up and down that he could see all kinds of perennial veggies growing in it.

Have to take An's word for that. Devon couldn't tell a weed from a prize-winning veggie yet. An'd promised to explain it all, after they got moved into the three story, five-thousand-square-foot monstrosity of a Victorian farmhouse that they'd bought.

Devon was pretty sure he was going to be spending his time renovating the place instead of gardening, but that was cool. He'd rather work with wood any day over grubbing in the dirt. Still, there was way too much to be done and Devon was seriously looking forward to a break sometime soon-like.

He sighed as he studied the last three boxes out of their combined move. Six people moving into the same place. Six times the chaos and six times the boxes. Yeah, sure, Devon had the least out of all of them but that just meant that he'd convinced the others that his things could be moved in last. Which meant that now they were all exhausted and not helping him.

Granted, they *had* chosen the hottest day of the summer to finish the move. Yesterday it'd been grey and cloudy, a nice sixty-eight all day long, but no, they couldn't start moving things yesterday, Friday. It had to wait for Saturday and a spike into the nineties. He sighed and scrubbed his face again with the already-sopping hem of his T-shirt.

At least they'd gotten the majority of the boxes into the house. Soon they'd all, Devon especially, be able to collapse for a bit. Devon hefted the one box of books left with one arm and then wrangled the box of silverware, assorted glasses wrapped in newspaper and potholders onto his shoulder. Sooner in, sooner done and damn it all, he wanted to rest.

"Dude, gimme that," Noy complained as he caught Devon on the stairs. "What the hell?"

"One box left," Devon said, dodging Noy's attempts to grab the silverware box. "Go get that one and shut the van up. Where're the others?"

"In the kitchen arguing about cabinets," Noy said. He rolled his eyes and headed for the van. "Good luck getting them to stop. Apparently where to put the plates is a Very Big Deal."

Devon groaned.

As the only person with good silverware—a legacy of his Grannie after she'd decided he needed a full set before he'd even hit junior high—Devon's set was the only one in the house. He already planned on buying more. Eight forks was a ton when you lived alone. Eight forks spread between six guys was going to be enough for one meal. If he was lucky.

Plates? They had enough plates to supply a mid-size army. Everything from formal china bought in Japan that An had brought to the house to Hanne's cheap blue army plates that would be good for camping but not for much else. The pots and pans weren't half the battle that the damned plates had become. Between the six of them, they had a proper number of pots and pans. Those plates, though, they were going to take over the kitchen if they weren't careful.

"You assholes better not be getting into a war over the plates," Devon shouted once he kicked open the front door.

The startled silence from the kitchen told him the answer to that one. In that silence, the house was perfect. A calm oasis in the middle of a lovely green yard. Sure, filled with boxes stacked on three different sofas and catawampus bookshelves that Devon was absolutely securing to the walls once he'd fixed the wainscoting, cleaned everything to within an inch of its life, and painted the living room.

"We do not need metal plates!" An declared the next moment, driving Devon to groan while Hanne spluttered in the kitchen.

Five hundred square feet of kitchen and it felt cramped. Devon shook his head at the others. What a mess. Six boxes sat open in the middle of the kitchen floor. Someone, probably An, had shoved the butcher block against the French doors that opened onto his kitchen garden. Great kitchen, tons of cabinet space, four very angry men filling it entirely.

"They're practical," Hanne complained. "I use them all the damned time."

An was five foot six and bristling with outrage. His gorgeous lean build and South Asian darkened skin contrasted delightfully with Devon's pale bulk. He could spend all day looking at An. And gladly would, if there weren't so many boxes to unpack.

Hanne was like cedar, tall and solid, muscle thick through his arms, legs and torso. With hair so blond, his scalp burned when he spent more than three minutes in the sun. Sunburns had already turned his scalp, cheeks and nose scarlet despite having been shoved into the house to unpack things about ten minutes into the move today.

"For camping," Devon said as he set his box of kitchen stuff down. The books went by the door so he could put them in his bedroom later. "Not for day to day. At least not anymore. And An, we're not eating on fine Noritake China every day. I'd spend the whole time afraid to move for fear I'd break the damned things. Special occasions are cool. Camping or, you know, cookouts in the backyard the metal plates are cool for. But day to day, we need good sturdy stuff that'll handle me and Noy slinging 'em around."

An flinched at the thought of Devon and Noy handling his Noritake. Completely justified there, even if it did make Devon want to rub his back and comfort him despite having put the flinch there. Hanne looked triumphant for all of one second before Devon glowered at him.

"I like my blue mug," Hanne grumbled.

"Fine, you get to keep your blue mug," Devon said. "But not the plates and bowls. Those are going in one of the top cabinets, out of the way."

He rolled his eyes as Placide pursed his lips and Suman hummed nervously, clearly unwilling to wade into the perpetual battle between An and Hanne. The two of them drove Devon nuts on a regular basis on that front even though they were good guys. At least they knew how to cook. Lord knew, Devon wasn't going to cook every single meal they all ate.

"He gets his mug," Devon said, wagging a finger at Suman whose lips curled in an unwilling smile. "An, I already got an angle on a china cabinet. It'll fit perfectly by the back door. Nice glass and everything for you to display the china but still keep it safe."

An breathed in so sharply that it was just the other side of a gasp. His scowl disappeared into a beaming grin that flashed those perfect, white teeth at Devon. As An did a victory dance right there in the kitchen, hips gyrating and wiry arms victory-pumping, Devon's heart just about leaped through his chest. How the hell was he going to live with An without embarrassing himself on a daily basis?

"Thank you!" An declared with a stabbed finger straight at Hanne. "You can have the damned blue mug if I get my china cabinet."

"Fine," Hanne groaned while rolling his eyes and lying through his teeth since he was the one who'd pointed out the listing to Devon a couple of days ago. "You get a china cabinet. I don't even fucking know what a china cabinet is, but you can have one. Can we please just put the plates away now?"

"Yes, we can," An said.

He and Hanne promptly cooperated like they were best

buddies, which they were when they weren't tearing each other's throats out, putting all the plates and bowls and then Devon's silverware away. Nice logical locations, too. Devon watched from the doorway and nodded.

"I don't know how you do that," Placide murmured once An and Hanne were deep into optimizing cutlery storage with little trays made out of bits of cardboard, taped together with duct tape.

"I am so replacing those," Devon grumbled. He blinked when Placide poked his shoulder. "What? I am. Cardboard. That's ridiculous. It won't take much to get some nice cedar, plane it down smooth, make some custom inserts for the drawers."

Placide shook his head. "Only you, Devon. Only you. What else have we got?"

"Oh, boxes are all in," Devon said, hooking a thumb over his shoulder towards the living room where Noy and the last box were waiting. "I'm all for crashing once I've got my last box of books to my room. We need a break."

Both An and Hanne looked up at the word 'break'. They looked at each other, nodded once, and then abandoned their work and headed into the living room. Placide followed them. Suman was already there with Noy and the last box from the van. The two of them muttered together as they set up the entertainment center with about six too many game systems, plus the monster 4G TV that Noy'd contributed to the house.

"Break time," An announced. "Devon declared it."

"Thank fuck," Noy groaned as he rolled onto his back

and lay spread-eagle in the middle of the floor. "Someone get me a beer."

Devon snorted, hefting his box of books and toeing Noy's foot as he passed. "Get it yourself, you doof. I'll be right back down. Just want to get my books upstairs. Maybe clean up a little, too."

Noy groaned, like moving would be far too much work, even for beer. Of course, Hanne went to get him one while Placide flopped on the couch and Suman started nudging Noy's side with his toes.

Dorks, all of them. His dorks, though, thank goodness. Living with them was way better than living alone ever could be.

Devon shook his head and headed up the staircase. It wound around the center of the house like a scrolling wooden spine made of polished red cedar and black oak. The black oak and cedar risers contrasted beautifully against the white-stained wainscoting that filled the house.

Whoever'd built the thing had dedicated a huge amount of time to it. Every riser had delicate oak leaf carvings in the center. The railings were individually turned and the banister was one continuous piece of laminated and sculpted red cedar that flowed sinuously down the stairs. Devon smiled as he ran his hand over it gently. Still sturdy. One of the few things he wouldn't need to fix.

His room was on the very top floor, up in the attic. Biggest room in the house if you counted the floor. One of the smaller if he only counted the amount of space he could stand upright. He fully planned on filling the lower portions of the room with built-in bookshelves and cabinets, just all the storage in the world. But for now, it was awkward, roof swooping around the sides of the room and paint scuffed and dented in so many places from the junk that had been stored up there.

The previous owner had said it was haunted, which was nonsense. There'd been a bat and some mice but getting rid of them had been easy. It'd taken Devon all of ten minutes to fix the holes that the critters got in through. Another hour to clean up all the mess, but that was expected.

Now it was just a big open place with boxes of books, a wardrobe and his bed off to one side. He was gonna need to put that bed together tonight if he wanted to sleep, but for now, the mattress and box spring sat on the floor and the frame was in pieces on the far side of the room.

Devon dumped his books to dig into his wardrobe which someone, probably An, had already filled with clothes. Clean dry T-shirt, clean dry flip-flops, thank fuck. His feet could finally cool off after all the hauling. And clean dry utilikilt because damn it, he was hot and a breeze below was just what he needed.

"We're... uh, ordering pizza?" An said from the doorway just as Devon dropped his sweat-soaked shorts and boxers.

"Sorry," Devon said as he stepped into his kilt and then pulled on his new Heavy Metal band shirt. Necrophagist, this time, still black, only dry and clean. "Couldn't stand the sweat anymore."

"No problem," An said, though his voice came out way too high.

His cheeks were bright red when Devon turned to stare at him. Devon watched as An looked anywhere but at him, face going redder until his ears were blazing along with his cheeks. An cleared his throat and jerked a thumb back towards the stairs, trying to say something but nothing coherent came out.

"Yeah, pizza with another pizza on it for me," Devon said while frowning at An. "Thin crust? I mean, depending on where they're getting it from."

"Sure," An said. He fidgeted in place like a little kid doing the potty dance, pointing back at the stairs. "Sure, yeah, that's great. I'll go... tell them that."

An darted off down the stairs, thundering down them like an elephant despite his size. It took a moment for Devon's exhausted brain to catch up with reality. Then he choked and stared at the top of the stairs.

"No way," Devon murmured, hands shaking on the waist of his utilikilt.

He heard the others talking downstairs. Sound carried up the stairwell perfectly. It was like a sound box, carrying noise all through the house if the doors were open. The others were razzing the hell out of An for his blushing and fumbling.

"Dude, just hit on him already," Placide said in a tone that normally wouldn't carry, but wafted up the stairs perfectly in this house. "You know he's queer. He's always staring at you."

"And Hanne," An countered in that too-high, almost frightened tone. "And Suman. And you. Even Noy sometimes."

"Oh, fuck you, he totally stares at me all the time," Noy complained, only to laugh as the others threw things at him.

Pillows, paper, hard to tell from up here but it sounded like they half buried Noy who just lay there laughing at them all for it. All the while, Hanne telling Noy that he had no chance against An because Devon was totally smitten with An.

Which, totally not wrong. Not wrong at all. Just… An liked him back?

"No. Way," Devon whispered as he shut his bedroom door. He leaned against it, heart pounding.

Devon bit his lip. An liked him? Like, for real, actual facts, liked him? As in wanted to fuck him, liked him? Christ, how long had that been going on? And why hadn't Noy told him? Noy knew how clueless Devon was about romance. Normally it took a club to the back of the head for Devon to catch on. And, well, that'd been just about a metaphorical club to the head, so maybe Devon was right on course for his normal cluelessness.

A quick trip to the bathroom one floor down to wipe off the worst of the sweat gave Devon time for his face to stop burning. And his kilt to lose the obvious tilt it'd acquired after An fled the attic.

Devon stared at himself in the mirror over the sink, trying to make himself believe what he'd heard. An wanted Devon. Liked him. Maybe? No, the guys had been serious about it behind the razzing and poking Noy for his ego.

An liked Devon.

Holy shit.

The house was quiet, aside from the normal creaks and pops of an old house baking in the sun, by the time he convinced himself to open the bathroom door. Devon stood on the landing of the beautiful stairs, biting his lip before slowly heading down.

The others were outside when he got downstairs, all but An and Hanne, who were nowhere to be seen or heard. Outside, Placide was half-heartedly wrestling with his ancient grill while Suman and Noy set up the lounge chairs that Suman had donated to the cause. Really old lounge chairs that probably weren't going to last more than a week or two.

"Dude, those are trash," Devon said as he watched Noy try to set one of the chairs up. The legs were bent and the seat fabric was torn. "Give it up."

"Yeah, true," Noy said, staring at the thing. "Don't have much else to sit on, though. The house is still a mess."

Devon nodded. "Not a bad idea, honestly, just not gonna work with that hunk of junk. Where'd An and Hanne go?"

"Pizza," Placide said with the little smirk that always,

always, always meant that someone, normally Devon, had missed something. "There's a good pizza joint in town but they don't deliver."

"Noy," Devon said, then waited until Noy actually met his eyes. "You're supposed to tell me when I'm being a clueless idiot."

Noy's jaw dropped open in a raucous cackle at Devon. "You finally figured out An likes you?"

"The stairwell's like a sound box," Devon said with a reluctant nod. "I heard you all razzing him."

Placide stared, face going red, then white, then red again. "I am never—ever—saying anything in the living room again."

He was so horrified that Devon laughed, waving off his horror. Couldn't blame him for that but seriously, it wasn't like they weren't already in each other's back pockets. The whole living in the same house thing would do that.

"Close your door when you want to be private and you're fine," Devon said. "It's the stairwell itself that does it."

No surprise, given that it was Placide's ferocity, Noy's love of lazing about and Suman's curiosity, the three of them immediately headed back inside to test the whole thing out. Devon snorted and let them go. Better to stay outside, toss those garbage lounge chairs and figure out something that'd work for an outdoor dining area.

He'd really like to have a covered porch, maybe screened, but that was a big project that would have to wait until after he'd fixed everything inside the house. Right now? Well, there was a nice gravel area by the back door and the last owners had left a bunch of hardwood tree trunk rounds that were just the right height for stools.

Devon shrugged. He had half an hour or so before An and Hanne came back with the pizza. Lord knows, the others would get distracted inside and forget to come back out to help. They always did, which was fine. That just meant that Devon could set things up just as he wanted.

Devon rolled the tree rounds over to the gravel area. It was a good size for a fire pit once he'd settled the rounds around the outer edge of the gravel and smoothed it a bit with a chunk of wood someone'd tossed off in the grass.

He thought about it for a second as he took a break in the shadow of the farmhouse. If they did have a fire pit, they'd spend hours and hours out there when the weather was even vaguely appropriate. The sun was going to bake him dry but hey, it'd be a nice thing for them to share if he put in the work…

Devon shrugged, went and dragged over eight abandoned concrete blocks that had apparently been planned as the foundation for some outbuilding that never was.

They made a great circle for a fire pit, especially once he filled the hollows of the blocks with earth and gravel. His stomach growled like a jet engine revving up as he finished patting the gravel into the blocks.

"What are you doing?" An asked from the back door.

"Eh, fire pit and seating that Hanne will fully approve

of," Devon explained. "No fire. Too hot for that. But we've got it set up for when the weather cools off."

An raised an eyebrow, not a hint of blush or any signs of attraction on his face as he came down the rickety back stairs to study the setup. "Not bad. I thought we had lounge chairs."

"Those things?" Devon snorted. "Those are garbage. I tossed them. I'll make something better. Or buy something when I get my next paycheck. It's not like they're super-expensive at Walmart."

He caught An's hand when An turned towards the house. He didn't want to lose that opportunity he'd glimpsed up in his room. An went beet red, but he didn't pull away. If anything, he clung to Devon's hand as if afraid that Devon would pull free.

"Um, first off?" Devon said, knowing right down to his toes that the others had to be watching this from inside. "I um... like you. A lot. You just never seemed interested."

"...If that's your first thing," An asked with a suspicious glare, first as he looked toward the back door and then at Devon, "what's the second?"

"The stairwell is like a sound box," Devon said. "I heard all the razzing you got when you went back downstairs."

"Fuck." An's head dropped forward. He cursed under his breath, low enough that Devon didn't really hear it. "Fine. Thank you for telling me. Damn it all."

"I'm kind of glad," Devon said. He winced away from

An's glower. "Normally, Noy tells me these things. I'm terrible at seeing it. He didn't this time, so, you know, I'm kind of glad that the stairwell let me find out. I'd've bungled around not realizing forever."

He still wasn't sure that An wanted to have more than just a fuck. He could? Maybe. Devon always assumed that the guys he liked were down for sex but not much more. Most of the time he'd been right. But it was different with An. They'd already decided that they could live together. Hell, they had a whole support network there in the house with them. If something went wrong, they weren't stuck on their own, struggling. Devon absolutely wasn't going to worry about messing the whole live-together-on-the-same-farm thing up. Overall, they were all pretty stable guys. It would work out. Probably.

No, absolutely. Devon wasn't going to lose any of the guys, especially An.

So, Devon bit his lip and squeezed An's hand while his heartbeat pounded in his ears. "Those assholes are going to come charging out any second. Um. Do you… I mean, um, what are you interested in? With me?"

God, he sounded like a dork!

His heart about leaped straight out his throat as An stared up at him. Devon couldn't tell from An's face what he was thinking. The wide eyes, the way An's nostrils flared as he breathed in sharply, that could mean shock. Delight in the tiny quirk of his lips? Or amusement?

"You really are terrible at romance, aren't you?" An asked and thank fuck, his voice was solid amusement. Not a speck of annoyance to be heard.

"Yeah," Devon agreed, rubbing the back of his neck with his free hand. An still hadn't let his hand go. "It's never made any sense to me, no matter what I try. So…?"

"I've wanted to date you practically since the day I met you, Devon," An said with just a hint of exasperation. He snorted. "Come on. We'll talk about it after we eat. If we don't head in, Hanne will win the battle to use those damned metal plates and then I'll lose the battle for keeping them out of regular meals."

The word 'date' turned everything else An said into white noise. Devon could pick out words here and there but they didn't string together until An hit 'metal plates' and the practical part of his brain kicked in, letting Devon start moving again.

"I'll back you up on that," Devon said as he let An pull him back into the house. "But honestly, pizza on metal plates is a bad idea. It'd chill the pizza way too fast. Nothing worse than half-congealed cheese on a pizza. Did you say 'date' or was I imagining that?"

Devon's luck being what it was, awful, he said that just as the door closed behind them with all the guys clustered around the kitchen island and it's six pizza boxes. Every single head came up. Hanne's jaw dropped open. Noy stood still for about half a second and then he shouted and punched the air.

"I told you!" Noy shouted at Hanne. He punched Hanne's shoulder and then ducked away before Hanne could punch back. "I told you so!"

"Uh, I was just asking if I heard right?" Devon said in the squeakiest voice ever, damn it all.

"You heard right," An said. There was a wealth of amusement in his voice even if his mouth was one tight line slashed across his face and his cheeks were blazingly purple, red again. "We can discuss it later. Behind closed doors and without assholes."

"With kissing," Placide announced and then grinned at both of them. "Dudes, if there is no kissing, I will be profoundly disappointed in you. There should be kissing, especially after this long of a clueless courtship."

The pizza was right there. Logic said that food came first, then unpacking, then maybe talking. But Devon frowned as An scowled before slowly releasing his hand. He didn't want to wait to talk. And kiss. He wanted to do that now.

Because An was gorgeous.

Gorgeous and smart as hell and sexy and fierce and, well, of all of Devon's new roommates, An was the one that Devon most wanted to wake up to the next day. So, Devon drew in a breath and grabbed An's hand before he could march across the kitchen and get involved in serving up the pizza.

An's eyes went wide as Devon pulled him back, caught him with one hand on his hip and then bent to, way too hesitantly, brush a kiss over An's lips.

"Weak!" Noy shouted only to immediately get smacked with dish towels by Placide who'd been wiping plates clean and potholders snatched from on top of the stove by Hanne and Suman.

An laughed, his breath warm against Devon's lips. "I agree. You can do better than that."

"So can you," Devon said with a grin of his own. "Especially since I'm terrible at initiating things."

"Oh, really?" An said.

He raised an eyebrow and then wrapped one hand around the back of Devon's neck to pull him down into a ferocious kiss that just about sent Devon to his knees. Hot and wet with all the tongue that a man could want. The sort of tongue that inspired thoughts of skipping dinner and heading up to bed. Except that both of their beds still needed to be put together. Though Devon could do without all the razzing, applause and laughter from the others.

"Do you guys have to do that?" Devon complained once An let his lips go.

"Yep, definitely," Noy said. He looked delighted by them both, leaning against the counter with his chin on his hands and a big smile that went all the way to his eyes.

"Absolutely," Suman agreed.

"It's seriously about time that you two got together," Placide declared.

Devon laughed, shaking his head. "You're all assholes and I'm hungry."

"I'd've thought you'd be saying that you wanted to go to bed," An said with a sly little smirk as he glanced at Devon's kilt. It had a decided tilt again.

"No beds put together yet," Devon said with as innocent of a shrug as he could manage while blushing and hard as a rock, with his best friends and brand-new lover observing every bit of his humility.

It wasn't much of a success because they all, An included, hooted with laughter. And you know? That was fine. Better than fine, really.

Because An leaned against him as Hanne went for the metal plates only to be shouted down by Noy and Suman while Placide passed out paper towels so that they wouldn't have to do dishes. The pizza was still hot, covered with cheese that was just the right side of burn-your-mouth gooey, plus ham and beef and sausage and a dozen veggies that Devon wouldn't've put on a pizza, personally.

Devon leaned against the wall, watching the others snark at each other while eating pizza in their kitchen. In their home. All of theirs. He didn't have to hide or worry or pretend to be anything else because they liked Devon exactly as he was.

And An.

An smiled at Devon with his eyes narrowed just a bit, a wicked little smirk wrinkling the corners of his dark eyes in ways that set Devon's kilt back out of true. Yeah, there was a ton of work left to do and Devon couldn't be happier.

Bring on the heat. Devon was ready for it.

"LAIRD" IS A GENDER NEUTRAL HONORIFIC

by Tobi Mackay

HANNAH KICKED OFF HER WELLINGTON'S at the back door and let herself in. Voices echoed down the hall from the kitchen. One was clearly her mum, smooth and low, even in the comfort of her own home she rarely rose above an unhurried murmur. The other almost had Hannah turning tail and running back outside.

"Hannah, is that you?" Hannah's mother, Mhairi, called. She sounded a little ruffled and as if she was dearly wishing for a rescue.

She let out a sigh and closed the door behind her. "Yes, mum." She put her bag of sketchbooks and pencils up on the battered old chest of drawers that sat beside the door and walked into the kitchen.

Sat on either side of the table was her mum, and—"Jackie, lovely to see you," she said, lying through her friendly smile.

Jackie, in her prim and proper outfit, looked like she was gearing up to give a speech on the evils of liquor and speaking to boys. "Hannah, dear, was that you out painting?" she asked with a condescending tone.

Sending a quick look at her mum—who had sagged a little, likely from relief at no longer being under the watery blue and terribly sharp gaze of the local gossip-monger—Hannah decided to take the reins. "Oh no, not today. Today I was just sketching." She went on a monologue about the views, animals, ruins, and light quality that now filled the sketchbook at the back door. Any time Jackie tried to break in and comment, Hannah used her speech to roll over her words like a runaway steam roller down a steep hill. She knew it was best to cut Jackie off as soon as possible, that way she had less chances to say things designed to make others feel small.

It worked. Jackie seemed to get bored. After that, it was only a few minutes before they were waving Jackie off and gratefully retreating to the kitchen. Mhairi pulled her phone out of her pocket and rang her friend Cate from down the road.

"Hi, Cate, Jackie's got gossip and is determined to share it come hell or high water. It might be a good time to walk the dog," she said. There was a hurried goodbye from the other side of the line and Mhairi dropped the phone back into her pocket with a shake of the head.

Hannah let loose a snort, "And you're always going on at me for not being polite to people." She couldn't hold back her grin.

Mhairi rolled her eyes. "You say that, but she arrived over an hour ago and until you came back she didn't look like she was interested in leaving." She shook her head, her grey streaked, brown pony tail swishing with the force. "That woman!"

Hannah collected up the mugs and filled the kettle. "What was she wanting to tell you about, anyway?"

"The old Laird's wake is in a week. The estate's finally been settled and we know who's getting the island. It's going to the old Laird's grandchild, by way of the son who died skiing. Of course, we all knew it would, though Jackie tried to make out that it was news," Mhairi told her, summing up what had likely taken Jackie at least half an hour to say.

Hannah frowned and tried to call to mind the details of the Laird's family. Even when she had lived on the island full time they hadn't come to mind much. "Is that the one who keeps going after married men and causing scandals?" she asked finally.

"No, that's one of the cousins, I think," she shook her head, "they're an awfully big family. The one who's inherited is the non-binary one, has a job doing the accounts for charities, I think."

That at least rang a bell, in fact it rang a whole belfry. "Mal de Moray? They've inherited?" she asked, surprise making her voice sharp. She turned from the kettle to look at her mum.

"That's the one," Mhairi agreed. "According to Jackie, they'll be coming up from Edinburgh for the wake." She grinned. "And how exactly did you know the name of our new Laird?"

A blush started to heat the back of her neck and with a sinking feeling, Hannah knew her ears would be turning red. Her mum looked more gleeful with every shade she grew darker. "When they came out, it was a big deal, you know, so I guess I just remembered," Hannah said, trying and failing to sound blasé. She ran her fingers over the edge of a tile in the countertop, pretending to be incredibly interested in the way that the tile and grout stood out against one another.

"Oh, I'm sure that's all it is. Just the community interest of one member of the LGBTQ community hearing about another?" Mhairi said.

Hannah did not need to look up to know that she was smirking. "Mmmhmm." The tile was becoming all the more interesting as the flush started to move from her neck and ears to her cheeks.

"So it's not got anything to do with the fact that Mal de Moray is six foot two and built like a professional rugby player?"

That was oddly specific and made Hannah look up from her inspection of the counter top.

Her mum sat at the table with her phone out in front of her having very clearly just looked up the new Laird. Her eyebrows were raised and she was clearly ogling whatever picture had come up on the screen.

"Mum!" Hannah exclaimed, scandalised.

Her mother, never one to take shame from anything she did that embarrassed her daughter, snickered.

***

Hannah twitched the skirt of her dress, after coming home and returning to her usual wardrobe of leggings and jeans, she'd forgotten how to sit in order to make it fall where it was supposed to.

After a few more flips back and forth, her mum leaned over and grabbed her hand, pulling it over to her so that she could keep her from fidgeting. "Less of that, your skirt looks fine." She rolled her eyes at her daughter. The pair were sat in the back seat of the old car, their black clothes camouflaging them in the shadows there.

Hannah frowned a little. She closed her eyes, settled back into her seat, and took a deep breath. She didn't like having to move in big groups of people, and the wake was promising to have more people at it than any other event in recent island history. Essle was not a tourist trap and she had gotten used to having the beaches and moors to escape to when things got too hectic at the house.

"We won't have to stay there for long," John, her dad, said from the front of the car. "Since we've got to drive back to the other side of the island we can skip out once we've done a few laps and chatted to the usual suspects."

"Who's likely to be there?" Hannah asked. Unconsciously, the hand hidden by her body from the sight of her mum had found its way back into the black silky material of her skirt and she was smoothing it between her fingers.

"Well, I dare say Jackie will have rounded up half the locals, at least. And the archaeologists investigating the ring of stones up on the Northern shore might come, though I can't imagine they've got the clothes for it. But it won't be too jam packed, school's still on and plenty of people will be having to work today," he said, driving with the slow and steady speed of someone happy to let the event they're going to carry on without them. Hannah had gotten her preference for small groups of people and quiet from her dad.

Eventually they made their way from the small and rutted roads that served the crofts, to the main road which ran in a wiggly thread around the coast, before lurching from the only town on the island, Lesser Bradgar, up to Old Castle. Old Castle was the seat of the Laird's family, though it was only a castle under the most generous terms. An ancestor of the current laird, one with a sorry lack of foresight for tourist desires, had knocked down the castle that had stood there and repurposed the stone into building a squat mansion. It did have two towers, one at the back and one at the front, but they had been later additions from nostalgic heirs.

There were usually flags fluttering high from the towers, the blue and white of the Saltire over the front of the house and the British flag sat mostly obscured at the back, but today they had been taken down to half-mast for the solemn occasion.

A nearby field had been taken over for people to park in. John parked them in a good spot without too much mud before jumping out and offering them each a hand from the car.

Most of the other cars on the island were lined up in the field, Hannah noticed sourly, it was going to be busy.

They walked up to the house and followed the signs pointing them round the side of the building to the garden. Someone had thought it through and probably realised that having several hundred shoes of varying levels of muddiness tramping through the house would be a bad idea. She could sympathise with that. A marquee had been put up to cover the mourners, or more accurately their food, since a big spread had been put out. There were bottles of wine, red and white, clustered at one end and Hannah gratefully filled up a glass with some of the latter.

Looking around at the crowd, she saw the "usual suspects" as her dad had called them. The people who saw events like this as a chance to see and be seen. Jackie, of course, had somehow taken over a pseudo-hostess role and was holding court over by the mini sausage rolls. Looking at the decor, Hannah thought she could see her hand in it. The black table cloths and lilies had more of a goth wedding vibe than that of a wake.

The food at least, looked good. Balancing a black paper plate on one arm, she did the rounds of the table. She took the chance to say hello to the people she saw as she went past and more importantly, took advantage of the fact that they were eating so the amount of conversation was limited.

Supplies gathered, she retreated to a shadowy spot that

was out of the way. There, Hannah took a deep breath, then a sip of wine. Her eyes had fluttered closed when she had inhaled, but the taste of the wine had her blinking them open again. The wine was … "Much better than I thought it would be," she said aloud.

A low chuckle came from a spot a little further down the marquee.

Hannah jumped and swung round to see who was laughing at her comment. A blush roared through her when she saw that it was, in fact, Mal de Moray. In a kilt, white shirt and waistcoat. Even worse, she realised, feeling a little faint, they had rolled the sleeves of their white shirt up to reveal firmly muscled forearms.

She cursed her luck and tried to drag her wandering brain back to ground.

Mal de Moray stepped forward, their smile a little sheepish, "Sorry, I didn't mean to startle you. I'm Mal."

Showing an incredible control over her instinctive responses, Hannah managed not to say, *Yes, I know, no one's shut up gossiping about you since we heard about the wake.* Instead she gave a smile, set her glass and plate down on a nearby table, and held out a hand saying, "Lovely to meet you. I'm Hannah Mackenzie, I'm so sorry for your loss."

Mal took her hand and shook. Hannah had to fight to stop her knees shaking along.

Bloody Hell, she told herself, it's their granddad's wake, you can't be acting like this. Have some god damn dignity. Trying not to act like she was pulling away from them too quickly, she took her hand back.

"Your grandfather didn't visit very often, but I think everyone on the island had fond memories of when he did," she said, scrupulously avoiding saying why those memories were fond and at whose expense they had been directed. It was at least true that the old man, more wizened and sun burned than a raisin, had been kind. There hadn't been a charity on the island that hadn't had the odd fun run or guess the number of jelly beans in the jar contest helped along by a handful of notes from his wallet.

"Thank you. I must admit, when I came up to the island, I didn't think it would be as well attended." They looked around at the crowd who had yet to notice the pair still hidden in their corner. Their eyes settled on Jackie and a tiny line of a frown settled between their eyebrows.

"Your family is held with a lot of respect by the island, and we don't often get a chance to show it, so I think that's why a lot of people have come," she said, trying to justify what must, she realised, feel like an invasion by a bunch of strangers intent on eating and drinking them out of house and home. Or, castle and summer home, she thought drily.

"And it's got nothing to do with an overwhelming curiosity about what the new Laird is like?" Mal said, turning back to Hannah with a single eyebrow raised and a smirk.

The blush came back. "Well, yeah, we're a nosy bunch, it's true. We want to find out what you're like, what kind of Laird you're going to be," she said, trying to seem blasé as she said it with a shrug. "The last good gossip we had was when a sheep escaped into one of the trenches the archaeologists dug and refused to come out."

The side of Mal's mouth twitched and then they were laughing, "Oh god, please tell me they gave the sheep an appropriate name afterwards?"

"I'll give you two guesses and remind you that we are on an island with actual crofts and crofters, so they may be biased in favour of one particular famous fictional archaeologist," she said, laughing along. They had, she noticed, a very nice laugh.

"I haven't been up to the dig yet, have you?" they asked. Their eyes twinkling with glee over the sheep and her name.

"When it started, but I haven't been back to see what they've found," she admitted. "I've been a bit busy."

"Oh, a hectic night life is there?" They set their shoulder against one of the poles propping up the marquee and looked down at her.

"Not really. Though I do feel honour bound to go to the Rainbow Cocktail Night my aunt puts on at the pub every Wednesday. It's her way of trying to be supportive," she explained.

There had been a bit of a boost in numbers when the archaeologists had come for the summer, but mostly it was her and the regulars drinking along to sparkly pop songs by pre-turn of the millennium bands. The cocktails were good, though, and her aunt's heart was squarely in the right place, so she kept going.

Their eyes brightened at the implication, "Really, maybe I should go this week?" Their shoulders seemed to lose some of the tension that had been pulling them taught and some of the creases around their eyes disappeared.

Hannah realised that she was, for once, passing pretty well. She'd left off her riotous collection of pins for the day, and her shoes were a pair of black T-barred court shoes, rather than the Wellington's spray painted pink, yellow and blue, or her rainbow laced walking boots. She wondered if they had been worried they were going to be alone on the island, in the midst of people with an eighteenth-century idea of gender and sexuality? It was nice to lay their worries to bed, she thought.

A very cheeky inner voice also added that it would be even better to lay something else to bed. But she stamped down on that thought with a brief blink of her eyes.

Hannah attempted to play it cool. She did not entirely succeed. "I'll be very glad to see you there."

A flash of a white smile, "It's a date then," Mal said. There was a thunderous silence after that statement, one that refused to be ignored and demanded to be filled with words. Instead, after a few seconds, there was a crash from outside their periphery. Looking towards the noise, Mal let out an aggrieved sigh, their firm jaw tensing. "Sorry, I'd better go see what that was."

"Of course," Hannah replied. Mal left with a smile, turning their back to jog off in the direction of the crashing sound.

Hannah did her absolute level best not to stare at the way the back of the kilt was filled out and the way that the white shirt stretched over a very nice pair of shoulders.

Well, she didn't try that hard. Mostly by itself, her head tilted to the side as she admired the tartan clad arse jogging off into the distance.

"Oh yeah, just community interest. That's it. Nothing else," said a wry whisper.

Her shoulders slumped and she turned to look at her grinning mum. "You're never going to let me live this down, are you?" Hannah said.

"Nope," Mhairi said gleefully, "Now grab your food and your wine, we have to go rescue the Brie and cranberries from your Aunt."

Doing as she was told, she grabbed her plate and glass, and followed her mum. Walking through the crowd was getting trickier, people had apparently heard that the wine was good and had been indulging.

Looking out across the sea of black and tartan, her eye was caught by a pair of broad shoulders and collar-length deep black hair. Then, their eyes met. Looking down with a blush, Hannah sped up to meet her mum at the table. It wasn't that long, after all, until Wednesday.

FIRST DATE
by Sienna Saint-Cyr

MADAM LADRO PACED in front of the classroom with her pointer aimed at the facts typed in red on the screen. The numbers were significant, but I couldn't comprehend what she was explaining. All I could think about were her long legs. How her gray skirt was slightly too tight and about two inches too short. Her white blouse pristine, and the top three buttons were undone. I imagined her blouse bursting open in front of us, her breasts springing forth as they were suddenly free of their confinement. I squirmed in my chair uncomfortably and looked around to see if the other students suspected my sudden arousal. None seemed to be paying attention. I was just about to look back at the screen when Madam Ladro's voice rose and her words punctuated in a manner that sent a chill through my body.

I snapped my eyes to her instantly. She was looking straight at me... talking about yesterday's test... But I hadn't heard what *exactly* she'd said.

My cheeks flushed with heat.

"Ms. Ellis," she crossed her arms, "You will stay after class."

In the back of my mind, I could hear the other students saying 'oooo, someone's in trouble...' just as children would do, though we were not children and no one was actually making noise. Instead, the class filed out silently and I stayed in my seat. My heart raced. It felt loud, though I knew no one could hear it pounding.

When the last student left the room, Madam Ladro walked slowly to the door and closed it. I thought I heard the click of a lock. My heightened senses meant that each step she took echoed in my ears as her high heels clanked against the linoleum. It meant that I was pretty sure that click *was* the door locking. Her footsteps meant she was walking up behind me, but if the clanking hadn't given it away, her scent would have. Madam Ladro smelled like sex; that musky intense smell that lingers after someone has had a gratifying orgasm.

I felt a hand on my shoulder. Her long, thin fingers dug into my flesh.

"You have some explaining to do, Ms. Ellis."

"I, uh..." I fumbled for words.

"You what?" Her tone was hard. Demanding.

I knew what she wanted to know. I'd cheated on my test. I'd done so in such an epic fashion that I knew there would be no mistaking my disobedience. But was that what she was asking? What if I'd missed something important she said moments ago and I answered the wrong thing, then I'd be in trouble for both. My heart beat faster as my thoughts raced with possibilities.

"Leave your items here and follow me." Her tone was cool, calm.

Madam Ladro led me to the opposite side of the room where there was an insignificant looking door. I'd been in her class for two weeks and hadn't noticed it until now. The paint was slightly peeling and unlike the rest of her classroom, this door looked dirty. Dingy. Not like a door leading to anyplace I'd want to enter.

Madam Ladro turned to face me when we reached the door.

"Put your hands behind your head," she said.

I stared at her, confused.

Before I could speak or ask why, Madam Ladro reached her perfectly sculpted hand up and slapped my face. The sting and shock brought tears to my eyes. My cheek felt on fire. I couldn't help but let a couple tears fall.

She raised her hand again and I quickly put my hands behind my head.

"Hmm," she said. "Seems you *can* learn."

Madam Ladro turned away from me again and opened the door. She walked through and kept going. Unsure if I should keep my hands where they were, I did just in case, and followed her into what appeared to be an office with dark, chocolate colored walls.

Blood red leather chairs were the first items to come into focus. The chairs faced away from us and toward a deep mahogany desk with nothing on it except a lamp with a brown, glass shade. The dark colors, dim lamp, and scent of leather set a mood. I just wasn't sure what kind of mood Madam Ladro had aimed for.

"Put your hands down and sit." Madam Ladro gestured to the chairs and made her way around the desk, where she sat in a taller, leather chair.

I did as she instructed.

Madam Ladro stayed silent. In my discomfort, I glanced around the room. On the surface, it looked like a normal office. One used for writing or reading or doing business type things. But the moment my eyes found the wall decor, I knew this was no ordinary office. Floggers, a few canes, handcuffs, terrifying leather straps, all adorned the walls of her office.

My heart beat faster and I quickly looked back at Madam Ladro.

"Tell me why you're here." Her words still firm, steady, as she sat up straight.

I hesitated and squirmed. The cool leather of the chair rubbed on my thighs as my kilt lifted in my movement. I looked down at my boots, as though they held answers.

"My reasons were in my application, Madam Ladro." My words were shaky, soft.

"That's not what I asked you."

I swallowed hard. Everything felt loud. Amplified.

I took a deep breath and forced myself to meet her eyes. "I'm here to learn discipline. And...to meet someone with common *interests*."

"How do you plan to accomplish those things if you don't pay attention?"

"I..." I paused, unsure how to continue.

"Yes?"

"I was paying attention..."

"To the lesson?"

Damn, *she had me there.* "No, Ma'am." I looked down again.

"What were you paying attention to?"

Fuck. "I don't want to answer that."

Madam Ladro opened a drawer to her right and pulled out a stack of papers. She dropped them on her desk in front of me.

"Ms. Ellis, please read guidelines seven through ten for me."

I reached for the papers. My heart sank when I read what they were from; my application. I found number seven and began reading aloud.

"I agree to follow instructions and participate in class activities. I agree to complete homework and tests honestly. I agree to obey my instructor at all times. If I break the rules, I consent to..." my words faded as I reached the last line. I knew what it said. It was the reason I'd even signed up for this fucked up and bizarre class. *Punishment.* It was what I'd craved more than anything... someone to put me in my place, to punish me for my wrong doings. It was why I'd cheated. I wanted to be corrected so badly.

"I'm waiting."

I met Madam Ladro's eyes again and finished the words I'd memorized the day I learned about her class. "If I break the rules, I consent to correction and punishment in the following forms: humiliation, bondage, spanking, and sexual favors."

The words alone caused a stir inside me. I felt myself getting wet. It was extra obvious with Madam Ladro's dress code of a short kilt and no underwear. I didn't want to get my juices on her nice leather chair, but the more I tried to focus on something else, the more the wetness traveled down my thighs.

My hips moved side to side as I stared into her deep blue eyes.

"Now, tell me, what were you paying attention to?"

"You, Madam Ladro. I was thinking about you and your blouse being unbuttoned. I was thinking about your hips. Your thighs..."

"Thank you for being honest. But you still weren't paying attention, and that broke the rules."

"Yes, Ma'am."

"How else have you broken the rules?" Her tone was still firm, but sweet. Like the sweetest honey, sticky and trapping me in her.

"I cheated on my test, Ma'am."

"Yes. You did."

We both sat in silence. I didn't know what to say. What to do. She was so calm. Tall and confident. Her lips so soft and breasts still pushing out of her blouse. My thoughts drifted back to the moment I'd first seen her. She hadn't been dressed so sexy at the time. She'd been gardening, covered in dirt and wearing overalls, her long blonde hair in a messy bun, and even then I'd felt mesmerized by her.

Madam Ladro—Samantha—had moved two houses down from my best friend. We'd met one morning while I was picking my friend up for work. From that day on, I showed earlier and earlier in hopes of catching a glimpse of Samantha. Sometimes I saw her, most times not, and each time I saw her felt exhilarating. But it wasn't until I saw her on a flier at the local sex store that I realized the woman I'd been so blown away by *also* taught a crash course in Dominant and submissive relationships. I'd signed up instantly, albeit with a shaky hand. I've fantasizing about her since.

I closed my eyes and lowered my head. "Please correct my behavior, Madam Ladro?"

She let out a long breath, and put the papers back in her desk.

"Stand up."

I did as she instructed.

Madam Ladro walked around her desk and moved the chairs to the sides of her office. They screeched across the linoleum and it made my back tense. I stood up straighter and stayed facing her desk.

"Bend over," she demanded, pointing at the desk.

My heart raced again. Wetness running down my thighs. I tried to take a deeper breath as I bent over but I couldn't manage anything beyond shallow, fast intakes.

I leaned on my forearms. The desk felt cold against my skin. Madam Ladro left me there while she circled her office, seeming to look for a proper disciplinary tool. This was what I wanted, to be corrected, taught, made better... And now, I was about to get it. Not just in general, but from a woman I'd not been able to stop thinking about since meeting her.

A scraping noise came from my left and it sounded as though she'd picked her implement. Her heels clicked across the floor again as she made her way back. The realization of what was about to happen made everything inside me go quiet. Peaceful.

"One more thing," she said as she walked.

"Yes?"

"What do you say if you need me to stop?"

"Sparkle star, Madam Ladro."

"Very good."

She stopped to my right and lifted my kilt, resting it over my lower back and exposing my bare ass. I gasped, mouth opening slightly as she ran her hand across my ass, her nails sharp against my skin. I wanted to turn around and plant a kiss on her, thank her for making my biggest fantasy come true, but I stayed still instead.

"With each strike, you will thank me."

"Yes, Madam Ladro."

Only the sounds of our breathing filled the space. It was so quiet that the moment the strap cracked across my ass, I jumped from the impact as well as the sound.

"Thank you, Madam Ladro!"

Crack.

"Thank you, Madam Ladro!"

Crack.

"Thank you, Madam Ladro!"

She continued until I cried out, this time in pain as the strikes pushed me over my emotional edge. Tears spilled over and my chest shook as I tried to thank her. But I couldn't get the words past my sobs.

Everything felt so good and raw. My cries of pain and release did not slow her strikes.

I heard Madam Ladro walk back to where she'd picked the implement and then return again. She pulled by kilt back down and stood behind me, placing a hand on my lower back. Her touch sent a shiver of desire through me. And something more... safety.

"Thank you, Madam Ladro," I finally managed.

"You took your punishment well. You are a good girl."

I wanted so badly to drop to my knees and beg her to take me home. I wanted to kiss her, hold her, worship her. I wanted her to hold *me* too and cherish me.

Madam Ladro removed her hand. "You may kneel before me."

I didn't try to stand first, I merely scooted back and lowered to my knees. I was crying so hard I had to turn on my hand and knees before pushing back into a kneel before her. My body didn't want to rise up. So I stayed on my hand and knees for a moment, allowing myself to feel everything moving through me.

"Goodness," she said. "You have a lot to get out."

"Yes, Madam Ladro," I squeaked.

I finally pushed myself back and pressed my heels into my tender ass, and rose up before her. Madam Ladro moved closer and pressed my face into her stomach, lacing her fingers in my short, spiky hair as she did so. Her embrace felt right and her scent like a summer breeze. She held me until sobs slowed and I felt calm again, then she helped me up and returned to her chair.

"Pull up a chair," she instructed.

I did as she said and sat again. The leather felt soothing under my skin.

"How do you feel, Ms. Ellis?"

Just the thought made me want to cry again, but I kept myself composed. "Wonderful. I don't know how else to describe it."

"Wonderful because of my correction or wonderful because *I* was the one that corrected you?"

I shivered, and we locked eyes. "The second."

She nodded and leaned back into her chair. Her silence gnawed at me. What was she thinking? Had I said too much? Admitted too much? Minutes passed and my stomach twisted into knots. I didn't want to be kicked out of her class. That was the last thing I wanted.

Madam Ladro took a deep, controlled breath before speaking. "If you are to learn proper discipline and become a better girl, you must follow my rules. Your behavior has been bratty and I don't tolerate brats."

I cringed. I'd read such.

"I'm sorry, Madam Ladro. I didn't realize my behavior was that of a brat. I won't do it again. Please don't kick me out." I kept my eyes down as I spoke.

Madam Ladro fell silent again, seeming to be contemplating. She leaned forward, her tone lowering, "You may stay. My days of tolerance are over, however. You have six weeks to prove to me that you're a good girl. You will pay attention every class, complete all required work, and no more cheating."

I tried to suppress my grin, lest I come off disrespectful. "Thank you for the second chance, Madam Ladro."

"You understand I will be testing you?"

"Beyond written tests?" I looked up again, held tilted.

"Correct."

Now it was my turn for silence. What did that mean? Even if it was hard, I wanted to see her—stay in her class—so I met her eyes. "I will pay attention and follow your rules, Madam Ladro."

"Good girl."

***

Five weeks came and went, and each class Madam Ladro upped her temptation. The buttons on her blouses slowly revealed more of her breasts, her perfume got stronger, her skirts shorter and heels higher, and her bun...ever so tighter. She called on me often, pointed out every time I missed a question in front of the *entire* class, and I loved her attention.

Each week, a different student was asked to stay after.

And the following week, some of them did not return. I had no doubt her office had seen its fair share of attention and I wished each time that it was I she'd asked to stay behind. Not because of disobedience, but because I'd been *so* good.

Today felt harder than any other day, however. I didn't want this to be our last encounter. Plus, it was our final, and so far, Madam Ladro was late. I squirmed in my seat. This was unlike her. I tried to stay calm and not assume the worst.

I twirled my pencil as I looked around the room. There were only six of us left. Six of twenty. Sad indeed. I was just about to glance at my watch again when I heard the door leading to her office open. Madam Ladro stood in the doorway, nothing more than a thin, black, lacey bra and matching G-string underwear.

She marched around the room, heels clanking and echoing off the walls with each step. Heat filled me as I felt moisture build between my thighs. How in the fuck was I supposed to pass the final with her looking so delicious? This wasn't fair. I'd tried so hard to be good.

"Today, as you know, is your final," she began, standing perfectly tall and confident in almost nothing in front of a class of ogling students. "You will do well to remember your rules and keep your eyes on your work."

Most nodded, but didn't answer aloud.

Madam Ladro passed out the tests with an air of temptation. When she got to me, she leaned low, allowing her breasts to nearly brush my face. Even though today was the last day and I could've shoved the test aside and buried my face in her, I couldn't. I didn't want to. In the weeks that passed, I'd grown to care. I wanted to please her. I wanted her to notice me, to look up when up when I dropped off my friend each day. Obedience had surpassed my class time.

I swallowed hard and kept my eyes on my test.

"Thank you, Madam Ladro."

I couldn't see her, but I felt her smile.

When we reached the end of our class time, Madam Ladro collected the tests. "Thank you all. You've been a wonderful class. I will email you your final grades and any personal notes I have for you to be able to move forward with. I wish you all the best, and please, don't hesitate to check in and let me know how you're doing."

Check in? I could check in? Just the thought made my heart flutter. I felt myself grinning when I heard a sudden, "Ms. Ellis?"

I froze. I had to force my words out, "Yes, Madam Ladro?"

"You will stay after class."

"Yes, Madam Ladro."

My stomach twisted once again. Had I done poorly?

I fidgeted as I waited for the others to say their thank yous and goodbyes to her. They were taking *forever.* Finally, the last student left. Madam Ladro walked toward me, and I stayed in my seat, bouncing my legs under the desk to hide my nervousness.

"What time are you off work tomorrow?"

"Five." I heard the surprise in my own voice.

"You will arrive at my house by six tomorrow. There will be a key for you under the mat and a list of instructions on the counter." Madam Ladro stood again and walked around the side of her desk. "Stand."

I did so.

She appraised me. "You will wear your boots again, though ensure they are clean before coming in my house. You will also wear your kilt and a white blouse with the top three buttons undone. Do you have a white blouse?"

I nodded.

"You will be making me dinner. I will ensure that you have all the necessary ingredients."

My insides smiled.

"I believe you know where I live, seeming as though you pass my house five days a week. *Sometimes six...*"

Heat filled my cheeks and I looked at her feet. "Yes, Madam Ladro."

"Then I will see you tomorrow. You will learn of your final grade then."

I giggled. I never giggle. What was this power she held over me?

"See you tomorrow," I said. I packed up my items and headed home.

***

I parked on the street in front of Madam Ladro's house. Her house didn't reflect the powerful, professional instructor I saw in class. Sunflowers taller than me lined the front of a cheery yellow house with white shutters. Her garden perfectly groomed, every plant in an ideal location. It was clear that Madam Ladro possessed a great deal of discipline *in every aspect of her life*. The key was where she'd said it would be. I unlocked her door, wiped my feet well on the mat, ensuring every bit of dirt was off my boots, then entered her home.

Large picture windows filled her place with warmth. It was the exact opposite of her office, yet also still perfect, pristine. Nothing excess. The floors were an older style hardwood, some scuff marks and signs of wear, but glossed over as if to preserve their age and history. Golden walls, oak furniture, and a cozy crimson sofa occupied the first room.

A hallway ran down the length of the house in front of me and I saw that the kitchen was farther back and to my right. I set my jacket and purse on the bench by the front door and headed toward the kitchen. Normally, I'd take off my boots, but she'd said to clean them, so I assumed she wanted me to wear them.

Her kitchen smelled of freshly baked cookies, though I saw nothing of the sort. The countertops were a steely gray, with bright white cabinets and walls. In the window sat lemons with a few twigs still on them. The instructions and a bag of ingredients were in the middle of the island counter.

I glanced them over. Baked rosemary chicken, asparagus, and brown rice. Very healthy, and also blah... Nonetheless, I searched her cupboards for cooking utensils and pans until I located all the necessary items.

Then I retrieved the chicken and asparagus from the fridge and got to cooking. While I was focused, I didn't think much about where I was, but the moment all the food was cooking and I'd cleaned up, my curiosity got the better of me and I began to wander around her house.

There was a bathroom off the hallway near the kitchen, a mudroom in back, and upstairs there were three bedrooms. One with another office, though this one looked like it was for non-debauchery business, a guest room complete with fresh flowers and a guest book to sign, and then the third, *locked*. I knew it was her bedroom. It had to be.

I played with the handle a bit before finally giving up and heading back downstairs. My curiosity wasn't worth breaking in and losing this opportunity, so I was good. When I reached the last step, I saw Madam Ladro, right in front of me, staring.

"I..." I gasped, "didn't hear you get home."

"Of course you didn't. You were upstairs."

"I'm sorry. I know you didn't say I could go up there. I was just curious."

"I knew you'd wander. That's why I locked my door. Some things need to be earned."

Once again, my cheeks filled with heat. She was good at that.

"Shall I check on dinner?"

"I think that's a wise choice."

I walked, maybe a little too briskly, to her kitchen and checked the chicken. It wasn't quite done. The asparagus and rice were, however, so I set them to warm while the chicken finished.

"It's not quite rea—" I began, but she'd followed me into the kitchen and when I turned around, she was right behind me. I jumped, heart suddenly racing. "You startled me, Mad—" I began again, but she put a finger over my lips.

"You will refer to me as Sam tonight."

I nodded as best I could, but she was strong.

Sam leaned into me, pushing me back into the counter. Everything inside me felt on fire. I wanted to grab her, fall to my knees and worship her, drink of her honey, but I stood there instead, unsure how to proceed. She removed her finger and cupped my cheek in her hand instead. All the fire suddenly moving to my lips and moist pussy. I squirmed under her body's weight, the counter digging into my lower back.

I leaned into her, the hand on my face urging me forward. Her face was so close that I felt her breath across my skin, and my eyes closed instinctively. "Please, kiss me, Sam," I pleaded in a tone I'd never used before.

"You want me to kiss you?" She mocked me, yet in a way that only made my desire grow.

"Yes," breathed my word. "Please, Sam?"

Sam wrapped her other hand around my hip and pulled me into her. She kept a firm hold on my face too, and leaned into me further. My insides screamed, begged for her tender lips, but all that I released was a whimper.

Just when I thought I couldn't stand it any longer,

Sam's lips met mine, hard. Firm. Tender, yet crushing. I soaked her up, meeting her lips with my own ferocious response. I opened my mouth and let her tongue invade me. Penetrate me. And it felt so right.

She pulled me closer, possessively closer, and I loved it.

We kept kissing. Neither seeming to want to pull away. But Sam finally did.

I looked into her eyes, showing her the depth of my desire. My growing need to worship her in every way. I could hardly breathe. Could hardly focus as my eyes kept rolling to the back of my head. What was this power she held over me? I didn't know yet, but I knew I wanted to find out.

"That's enough for now," she said. "You have a dinner to finish and we need to eat. For now, set the table and I shall return after I've changed into something more comfortable."

"Yes, Sam."

I watched her as she walked away. I'd hardly noticed what she was wearing. I'd been too focused on her eyes, *her touch*. When she was out of sight, I took a few moments to regain my composure. Then I found some plates and silverware and set the table. It was a small table, round, sitting in front of a window in the back of the kitchen, but it was cozy.

By the time Sam finished changing, the chicken had finished cooking and I retrieved it from the oven. The rosemary smelled so good now, not at all how I remembered the herb smelling. I placed the chicken on the counter as Sam lit a couple of candles on the table.

We both dished up and sat, though I couldn't bring myself to take a bite. All I could think about were those tender lips and how they'd crushed down onto mine. The flickering candles illuminated Sam's face, making her glow.

Sam met my eyes. "Aren't you going to eat?"

I bit my lip. "Yes, it's just..."

"Just?"

I giggled, and looked at my plate. "This is the most exciting first date I've ever had."

Sam smiled. "Just wait..." Her mouth turned devious. "Later, I plan to take you into my bedroom and tell you about your final grade. You'll want to eat well, *trust me*."

I couldn't suppress my own grin as I took my first bite of the savory chicken. I imagined her bedroom holding the same delicious decor as her classroom office had. I squirmed as my excitement grew. This really was the best first date I'd ever had.

A GLOAMING ROMANCE
by Julie Ogilvy

CHAPTER 1

'Go to the wilds of Scotland' they said. Peace and tranquillity to finish your book; no interruptions, no noise or distractions. How wrong they were. Renting a small cottage on the edge of a small hamlet gave the occupants living in the twenty houses an excuse to see who the newcomer was. Bringing him cakes and stews as an introduction, the locals got his life story and he got no work done.

Brad Firman was hoping that at thirty-four he would get his first book written in a month; that was two years ago. Working a full-time job as a bar manager didn't give him a lot of free time to write. Saving every penny, Brad had managed to accumulate a few thousand pounds. Enough to take six months off to find his inner author and get his damn book finished. Two months down and he had only written two chapters. What with the meals and the constant interruptions his life was just as hectic as back in London. Evenings were spent being coerced by the villagers to spend time with them in the local pub, where they played dominoes, card games or darts. He had to admit the evenings were fun but they distracted him from his writing.

Waking up at 6 a.m. to take a solitary hike to an out-of-the-way beach, Brad packed food, his tablet and swimwear. Someone had drawn him a map showing the paths to take there and back. Whistling happily that today he would get time to himself without the kind-hearted folk, he loaded his backpack and set out for his adventure in the wild landscape.

CHAPTER 2

Gulls squawked as they argued over the seaweed scattered across the soft golden sand. It took Brad two hours to walk over the heather moorland to reach the beautiful deserted beach. He took his time, snapping pictures as he walked among the purple flowers and listened to the sounds of grasshoppers chirping and the birds singing.

Setting his backpack down, Brad looked at the vista opening up before him. Golden sand that stretched for miles was being lapped by a calm blue sea. The cresting waves gently breaking over the shore. The sound of the sea calmed Brad, lifting his spirits as well as putting ideas for his novel into his head. The two-hour trek over the heather moorland was worth the effort of putting his legs through the aches of his unexercised body. He swore he was going to exercise more. During the walk he had taken many photos of the landscape and a few selfies he was going to send to family and friends back home. The peace and silence were broken by the chirping of grasshoppers and birds singing, but it beat the honking of horns and all the other noise pollutions of London.

Now standing at the top of a sand dune, Brad looked around and realised he had never been so far from civilisation and alone in his whole life. It was exhilarating but also scary; he could be the last human alive. Screaming loudly to free his pent-up frustrations, Brad laughed knowing no one could hear him scream. Screaming again, he grabbed his backpack and ran down the sand dune, regretting it when he fell and ended up rolling down the last few feet. As Brad lay on his back, catching his breath, he felt like a teenager again with no adult worries to fill his mind.

Brad pulled out his laptop and let his imagination flow as he ate his lunch. Ideas came in a torrent, flooding his thoughts. He wrote everything down before he forgot; that was the worst, forgetting great plots or lines. Once he had finished, Brad stretched out on the warm sand, looking at the fluffy white clouds slowly floating in the blue sunny sky.

Smiling to himself, Brad decided to go skinny-dipping. He stripped off his clothes. The only audience he had were the birds and the sea creatures, who didn't give a damn if he wore trunks or not. Strangely, walking naked across the sand freaked him out. Why? He wasn't sure, but the thought that someone might see him jangling his bits, made him walk faster with his hands hiding his manhood.

Stopping suddenly when he thought he heard laughter, Brad looked around but all he saw was the empty beach and the dunes. He shook his head, putting it down to the wind playing tricks on him.

Running into the cold water took his breath away. Cursing loudly, he headed back to shore. Shivering and holding his somewhat smaller manhood, he ran back to his towel. After a quick rub down, he laid down his towel to soak up the sun. Laying on his stomach, enjoying the warmth, he was soon lulled by the silence. He fell into a deep sleep.

Water washing over his toes woke him up in a panic. Brad sat up with a start, forgetting where he was until another wave crashed over his legs. Brad dressed quickly, wincing when he stretched his arms in the air to pull his t-shirt on. Falling asleep under a hot sun without sunscreen was probably not the wisest thing he had done.

The tide was coming in quickly and he needed to leave. Grabbing his stuff, he walked in haste up the sand dune. Not an easy feat when he kept slipping backwards with the dislodged sand. Upon making it to the top, he cheered with happiness. He waved goodbye to the tranquillity of the beach and set off for home.

Twilight descended in a cloak of reds, pinks and tints of gold. Snapping pictures of the kaleidoscopic sky, Brad lost his footing in a rabbit hole, twisting his right ankle.

He fell hard on his front. Using words as colourful as the sunset, Brad rolled onto his back.

"Are you okay?" A shadow asked Brad.

CHAPTER 3

Brad stared open-mouthed at the tall Adonis standing over him. In the darkening sky he couldn't make out his features but his plaid kilt showed a gorgeous pair of muscled legs. Damn, why did the only man in this wilderness have to find him on his back with tears of pain streaming down his face.

"I'm fine. Thought I'd laze on my back for a while to soak up the twilight," Brad said, going for sarcasm to hide his embarrassment.

"Aye, the gloaming is beautiful tonight but it is also a dangerous time for people who like to laze on their backs," the shadow said in a sexy Scottish brogue.

"Dangerous? How?" Brad hoped he was joking.

"Do you know the way over the moorland in the dark? Once the sun dips below the horizon it gets dark quickly. Plus, there are wild beasts that prey on lost travellers. Have yea a name?"

"No, I guess I don't know the way in the dark. I've a map and a phone with a torch function. GPS, I suppose. I fell asleep. What kind of wild beasts? Are we safe? Oh, Brad by the way," he answered, feeling silly for being on his back and on the brink of getting lost.

"Finn. We're safe for now, but when the dark of night arrives, *run*. Can you even walk?" Finn asked while holding his hand out.

"I think so. Thanks," Brad winced when he put pressure on his foot.

Finn helped Brad sit down so he could put the backpack on his back. "I'll carry you. You may have broken your ankle."

"I'm quite capable of making my own way home thank you…. Agh!" Brad screamed as a small tongue licked his hand.

"Ross, come here. Good boy. Brad, meet Ross," Finn laughed, introducing his little Westie.

"Hello, cutie, sorry if I frightened you. You scared me. I thought you were a wild beast." Brad stroked the wee dog.

Brad stood. "May I have my backpack please?"

"Of course." Finn smiled, handing over the backpack.

"Bye, Finn, bye cutie." Brad stood tall and took a small step.

Walking a few more steps, he nearly fell back on his butt. A sharp pain ran through his ankle, making tears gather in the corners of his eyes. In a blink, his backpack was pulled from his back, hiked over Finn's back, and Brad found himself cosseted in the strong arms of his rescuer.

"I can feel the heat of your embarrassment pressing against my heart," Finn whispered.

"And now it is getting hotter. Thank you for taking me

home. How do you know where I live?" Brad blushed beetroot.

"I'm taking you to my cottage. It's nearer and though you aren't big, you will definitely become heavy before getting halfway home. I take it you are the author living in Ivy cottage."

"Er... um... yes, I am. Talk of the town. I haven't seen you around." Brad would definitely remember a beautiful hunk like Finn.

"I only go into town when I need to replenish my supplies. People living in the hamlet love to gossip in the aisles of the supermarket. Having one supermarket covering a large area with small villages and hamlets, gossip is the biggest pastime for folks visiting the shop. Someone coughs and by the end of the day they have the bubonic plague.

"You, my dear Brad, are the main topic since you moved in. Everyone wants to know your story. Are you running from a broken heart? That is winning by a margin, followed by, you left your bride at the altar," Finn surmised.

"Haha! I told everyone I came up here to write a book. No broken heart. No bride left at the altar, although it would be a groom. No mystery, I'm just a man whose dream is to finish my book." Brad laughed nervously.

Mindful of every muscle underneath him, Brad surreptitiously pressed his body into the hardness carrying him. Wrapping his arms tighter around Finn's neck, Brad let his head fall into the warmth offered by Finn's shoulders.

***

"Earth to sleepyhead, we're home. Welcome to my abode," Finn said whilst waking Brad up. Finn blushed after calling his home theirs.

"Home," Brad said, happy to be going home with someone. Realising what he said, Brad tried to stand, "I mean your home and obviously not mine."

"It's okay. I knew what you meant. Can you turn the door handle, it's not locked," Finn replied, sounding a little dejected.

Brad did as he was told, but wondered if he'd hurt Finn. Had he upset him? He hoped not. When he woke up, Brad was the most relaxed he'd ever felt. Finn's words washed over him in a blanket of security and he revelled in Finn saying 'we're home'. He cursed his sleep induced mind, giving him hope of romance with the gorgeous man.

After sitting Brad on the dining table, Finn removed his shoe and sock to assess the damage. It was swollen with a nasty large bruise forming. "I don't believe it's broken, just badly sprained. I'm going to wrap a bandage around it. Hopefully, the compression will alleviate the swelling."

"Thank you," Brad said, looking up at Finn with a hint of a smile and a sure gleam in his eyes.

Finn looked at Brad with the same lust shining from his eyes. Taking the first step, Finn edged closer, lifted Brad's chin, and kissed him. When their lips met, Brad felt goosebumps tickle his heated skin and his heart somersaulted. A tentative kiss with promises of more to come. Brad wrapped his arms around Finn, pulling him closer, intensifying the kiss with demands of his own. Finn pressed his lips harder, silently asking for entry, Brad responded, allowing their tongues to dance together.

Brad's mind blew with the sensual touches Finn's lips and hands were causing; his body trembled as it responded to the sexual pleasures given by Finn. Stroking his hands over Finn's body, Brad grabbed his butt through the thick kilt, almost coming when he didn't feel any underwear. Lifting the kilt, he groaned into the kiss as he caressed the soft naked butt.

"Do you want to go to the bedroom?" Finn murmured sexily into Brad's ear.

"Yes," Brad panted.

Carrying Brad upstairs, Finn thanked his lucky stars he was walking over that piece of moorland to find Brad. Laying Brad on the bed, he undressed him slowly, kissing the skin as it became exposed. Brad lay panting on the bed, silently begging Finn to speed up. Removing Brad's boxers, Finn kissed his manhood, making Brad gasp for more.

Finn stood and kicked off his hiking boots, tossed his socks, ripped his shirt off and was unbuckling his kilt when Brad stopped him. Reaching out his hand, Brad pulled Finn on top of him.

"I love your kilt, especially knowing you go commando. A plus for outdoor activities," Brad winked.

"Aye, you would look grand in a kilt, sitting on my lap while I have my wicked way with you in the heather. Something I've never had the pleasure of doing with anyone yet," Finn said, seeming to see the slightly jealous glint looming in Brad's blue eyes.

"I'm not really jealous but the thought of being the first to play with you in the heather is very sexual and endearing," Brad said, blushing like a teenager.

Unbuckling the black leather and silver buckled belt, Brad licked his lips at the perfect specimen on top of him. Finn's body carried the scars of living out in the wilds, of working the land. Hard muscles formed from hard work and not weights at a gym. Unable to keep his hand off him, Brad traced his fingers over the naked skin trembling under his touch.

That night both found heaven in the cosy cottage in the middle of nowhere.

CHAPTER 4

A wee wet nose pushing into Brad's armpit woke him up early the next morning. Jumping in fright, he landed his hand right on Finn's groin, causing him to scream in agony and curl into a ball gripping his tender parts. Ross barked, happily wagging his tail now both men were awake.

"I'm sorry, Finn. Ross scared the life out of me. I'm not used to having something wet and cold shoved into me as I sleep. How's your little man?" Brad stroked Finn's back.

"Okay. Little? You hurt me then insult my man," Finn croaked, trying to hide his pain.

"Not little in the least but it was said as a compliment. I hope to see your big man today."

"Hmm, well he might make an appearance when the ache has dispersed. Breakfast? How's your ankle?" Finn asked, rolling into his back grinning.

"It's still swollen but not as much. I think I may need to stay another day. Is that okay?" Brad asked cheekily, caressing Finn's big man that was getting bigger with each stroke.

"Stay. Don't stop," Finn begged.

Two hours later, they managed to make it out of the bedroom to shower. They showered so long, cold water rained over the two kissing men, forcing them out of the shower. Shrieking as the icy droplets cooled their heated bodies, Finn quickly grabbed warm towels. Hobbling on one foot, Brad was soon in Finn's arms as he swept him off his feet and onto the bed.

"Though your body is tempting, alas I must go to work. Animals need feeding and I need to check on the land. Feel free to do as you wish. I'll be back for dinner. First breakfast," Finn kissed Brad, reluctantly pulling away to dress.

"I can help you feed the animals. My foot isn't that bad."

"Aye, we'll see. Here you go. These should fit." Finn gave Brad a black t-shirt and a green tartan kilt.

Brad let Finn wrap the kilt around his waist as he

donned the t-shirt. Buckling the belt, Finn added a kilt pin to the lower part of the skirt. Brad loved the feeling of freedom, it felt a little weird not wearing underwear; which he soon forgot as they got breakfast.

After a quick breakfast of beans on toast and a strong brew of tea, Finn lead Brad to the barnyard. It was a small area with a stable, a barn and a pigsty. Two donkeys shared the stable with two horses. In the barn lived a medley of sheep, goats and alpacas. A large grumpy black pig lived in the small sty set in the corner of the barnyard.

"All the animals are rescued. People bring them here from all over. I give them sanctuary until someone adopts them. The six sheep are going to a petting farm tomorrow. The goats and the four alpaca I'm keeping along with Grumpy the pig. She is a miserable old sow who hates everybody, including other pigs and animals. We have an understanding, I leave her alone, she leaves me alone."

"Wow, they are all lovely animals. You are lucky to be able to care for them. Are the donkeys and horses yours?" Brad asked, feeding a small grey donkey a carrot.

"The donkeys have been here a month, they were going to a smallholding but the other donkeys shunned these two so they were returned. So aye, they have been adopted by Orion and Fudge, my horses."

"You named a horse Fudge?" Brad teased.

"Nay, a child who came to adopt a pony, named him Fudge because of his colour. I named him Apollo but the bugger prefers Fudge. Wouldn't come when I called out Apollo but ran back to Fudge. You have no sense, have you Fudge?" Fudge neighed in return, looking for another carrot.

"Don't listen to him, Fudge, it's a lovely name. So they are the only animals not rescued?"

"Yes. Ross is a rescue, I found him chained to a tree at the side of the road abandoned by his previous owners. Had him for eight years. Have you got pets?" Finn asked.

"No. My hours don't allow me the freedom to keep any. I love animals. One day I might have enough money to write full time so I can have a pet."

Finn herded the animals into a large paddock to frolic. Brad limped behind Finn, thinking on how he really should get his life back home sorted. Taking another step, he nearly went head over heels when Grumpy stopped in front of him, giving him a once over.

"Sorry, Ms. Grumpy. I didn't see you there. You are looking very beautiful today." Brad smiled, reaching out to stroke behind her ears.

"I wouldn't...." Finn started to warn, but he was silenced by Grumpy accepting the petting. "Well I never. You are honoured, Brad."

"She is beautiful. Misunderstood, aren't you, Ms. Grumpy," Brad said proudly, stroking the pig.

"Humph," Finn grumped.

Laughing, Brad led Ms. Grumpy into the grassy paddock. Once all the animals were securely inside with the gate firmly closed, Finn grabbed his shepherd's crook, then kissed Brad with a passion that took the breath out of a stunned Brad. Misty-eyed, Finn left to work the land.

"Wow, Ms. Grumpy, that was the best kiss ever. Finn is drop-dead gorgeous. Don't you tell him," Brad confided in the pig snuffling in a muddy patch.

Realising he was talking to a pig, Brad decided to head back to the cottage. For the second time in a while, Brad had the urge to write. Brad grabbed his tablet and a chair from the dining room and found a sunny space in the barnyard to start his new book.

CHAPTER 5

Finn checked the new saplings he planted earlier in the spring. Twenty Douglas firs to replace the trees he cut down to make garden gates and animal carvings. Selling his creations paid for the upkeep of the rescue animals and his home. The saplings were in good shape, growing daily, in spite of being attacked by deer and squirrels who devoured the bark and nibbled the new shoots. By checking the saplings and encouraging the wildlife to eat in a different part of the woodland, Finn managed to save most of his new firs. Caring for the land was mainly achieved by trial and error. Finn loved the challenges his work offered him.

Today, the land couldn't hold his thoughts, a certain author was occupying his mind and filling his body with sexy intentions. Rushing through his chores, Finn made his way home. Walking into the barnyard, he smiled seeing Brad leaning against Grumpy, writing. He was nodding his head to a tune only he could hear through his earphones.

"Hi sexy," Finn said, making Brad jump.

"Hi yourself. Finished?" Brad asked, removing the earphones.

"Aye. My mind was distracted. How the hell are you still alive? Grumpy has not once allowed anyone to touch her. Have you, old girl?" Finn said, sitting next to Brad only to have Grumpy snort at him.

"Insulting a pretty lady isn't going to endear her to you. Who's a pretty piggy?" Brad said, tickling her ears.

***

The afternoon sun beat down on the couple making out in the heather behind the paddock. True to his word, Finn took Brad while he sat on his lap with his kilt splayed out around them. In the distance, if they bothered to listen, the sea was breaking over the sand while herring gulls squawked as they gathered on the beach for an afternoon feast.

Sated, they lay gently caressing, not wanting to let go of each other, not quite yet. Their kilts were the only clothing they wore, which teased and added a mystery to what was hidden beneath its pleated fabric. Brad loved to run his fingers over the plaid to feel Finn's gorgeous bum begging for his touch. He never would have guessed he was a kilt man. Brad used to think a butt encased in denim was a turn on but it didn't hold a candle to Finn in his kilt.

"You're so sexy. The debauched look suits you. Your kilt in disarray is super sexy," Brad whispered across Finn's lips.

"Hmm..you look just as wanton. A rakish rogue on a

mission to deflower a fair maiden," Finn teased.

"So you are my fair maiden. I think I have deflowered you, maybe I should have another go, for good measure. I'd hate to leave you with your virtue," Brad said in a deep sexy voice.

"Oh please kind sir, take my flower. It is a burden to carry," Finn replied in a high-pitched imitation of a young girl.

Laughter soon turned to sighs and moans as the two men found pleasure from making love. The late afternoon sun began to lower casting long shadows over the wild heather, creating a mystical landscape.

"Time to put the animals to bed," Finn said, pulling Brad from his blissful reverie. "You were away with the fairies."

"The only fey I'm away with is you. It's so peaceful. I don't think I have ever felt so relaxed in the silence of a place. The traffic is a constant buzz back home," Brad mused.

"That would drive me mad. How can you cope with the noise pollution?"

"My mind switches off the noise. One gets used to the background buzz. You'll have to come visit."

"I'd like to see your habitat. Brad in his urban home. Piggyback?" Finn asked.

"Please," Brad smiled, jumping on Finn's back.

Helping Finn round up all the animals, Brad thought it an idyllic place to live. That day he had written six chapters in his book and his mind was still being plagued by ideas; mostly about Finn and his farm. Watching Finn guide a snorting Ms. Grumpy into the barnyard, Brad stopped in his tracks. His heart beat fast and his breath stopped, could he really be falling in love with Finn in less than a day. The thought of leaving him made his insides weep at the loss. Shaking his head to clear the silly idea of love, he helped put his favourite pig into her sty.

Finn led Brad through the barn to a studio built on the side. Opening the door, he let Brad step inside first. Brad turned in a circle, taking in the wonderful creatures around the room.

"Bloody hell, Finn. They are magical. Just wow!" Brad was speechless.

Carved wooden animals; bears, badgers, foxes and many more were expertly recreated in wood. Garden gates with intricate designs incorporating flowers, trees and leaves leant against the walls. Most of the artwork had sold stickers on them.

"Thank you. This is my true passion. This is my living," Finn said quietly; it was the first time he had allowed anyone to enter his den.

"I'd buy them all if I had the money."

"I'd give them to you, if I didn't have to make money," Finn laughed. "Before dinner, would you like to sit and watch the gloaming over the sea? If your foot is okay."

"I'd like nothing more and my foot is feeling a lot better. I always have you to carry me back home," Brad said.

***

Sitting on top of the sand dune, wrapped in each other, they watched as the reds, oranges and purples turned to the evening blues and darker shades of night. Ross chased the gulls across the sand in the hope of catching one. Brad and Finn needed no words to know that they were happy and falling in love.

EPILOGUE

"Hurry up, Brad," Finn shouted to his husband.

"I'm coming, hold your horses. My damn kilt blade is stabbing me," Brad shouted back.

Finn came to his rescue. "It's not a damn blade it's a sgian dubh, a tradition knife. You are supposed to keep it in its sheath."

"I know. I wanted another kiss before we face everyone. I love you husband," Brad said, and kissed Finn.

"Hmm…As seductive as you are laying on our bed, our guests are waiting," Finn said, caressing his husband's butt under his dress kilt.

"Spoilsport. Whose idea was it to invite family and friends to a blessing?"

"Yours, my dear husband. I love you too," Finn teased.

Earlier that morning they got married at the registrar's office in front of their parents. A quiet, intimate affair, which was everything the two could wish for. Exchanging rings, Finn was glad he wasn't the only one that had a tear or two. Brad kissed them away, as Finn wiped Brad's with his thumb. Laughing at their emotions, they embraced for the first time as husband and husband.

Now they were getting a blessing on the beach with all their family and friends. Standing on the sand with the sea gently lapping at their feet, Brad and Finn said their vows. Wearing their kilts of green tartan Brad and Finn made a striking couple. White Jacobean shirts finished their outfits. Purple heather buttonholes pinned above their hearts, made by the couple from the moorland they loved so much.

Seeing Finn in his kilt, showing off his gorgeous legs made Brad's heart swell with love and joy. He found more than his words coming to the wilds of Scotland, Brad found his kilted soulmate.

Finn stared at his husband through eyes brimming with tears of love and happiness. His soulmate with a penchant for kilts, literally fell at his feet. Never in his wildest dream did he image loving someone would be this thrilling, romantic and exciting.

Fairy lights lit the path back to the barnyard where tables were set up with food. Waiting until everyone had departed the beach, Brad and Finn danced as the twilight colours set the sea on fire.

"I'm so glad you found me laying on my back with my injured ankle. I love you, Finn. Though I know now it was you who laughed at me running naked that afternoon."

"You looked stunning in all your naked glory. I wanted nothing more than to find you and ask you for a date. I love you, Brad. Hard to believe a whole year has passed by."

"You told me to stay that first day, so I stayed. Best decision I made," Brad smiled.

Ross ran towards them carrying a book, his tail wagging excitedly. "Ross, come here boy," Finn called to him.

Ross ran past the couple, dropping the book in the sand when a gull cried overhead. Finn picked up the book, holding it tight. He was so proud of Brad getting his book published. 'A Gloaming Romance' was based on their love.

"Well Ross isn't enamoured by my book. Trying to drown it at sea," Brad laughed.

"He thinks rolling in fox poo is the greatest pleasure in life. Maybe he was offering it to the sea to give his blessings to our marriage. It was here that the magic of our romance began." Finn lifted Brad into his arms.

"True. To us and the beautiful gloaming."

THUNDERHEART
by Gregory L. Norris

ANOTHER OF THOSE HAUNTING DREAMS played out, like a music video made within my imagination, meant only for me. Sting was singing about building a fortress around my heart, but instead of gyrating in his bare feet and working his guitar like it was a musical extension of his tantric cock, I was there again, standing outside the castle. Thunderheart's castle.

The deepest of emotions possessed the specter of my dream-self: arousal and a breathless sense of anticipation fighting against fear, and, yes, above all else, love. As I gazed up at the gray stone fortress surrounded by green countryside, the castle intact once more in the territory of my subconscious, tears jabbed at my eyes. Breathing came with difficulty, and I sensed without first moving that I'd gotten erect. I was beyond hard, in a state verging on painful. All because I knew *he* was there, inside those gray walls surrounded by green, and he was waiting for me.

"Thomas," I gasped, though my voice emerged barely

above a whisper, which the country wind in Scotland's dark past soon carried away. *"Thunderheart!"*

Motion stirred, a shadow visible through the cross-shaped archer's arrow loop stronghold formed by the stone blocks in the upper chambers of the castle's eastern bartizan. My heart attempted to jump into my throat. I choked it down, gulped a sip of damp air, and smelled roses. Then I was running, aware of the grass underfoot slick with new rain, and his voice, calling to me from within his keep at Castle Balglamis.

"Here, Jesse!" the warrior beckoned.

Crows took flight in the surrounding woods. A rumble of thunder cleaved the heavy air. The murky gray hanging over the castle broke with a flash of hot silver light. Through a kind of second sight, I knew he would circle down the east spire's stone staircase. I raced through the wishbone-shaped arch that connected the two halves of the castle into a stone courtyard set before a postern—that imposing door of oak the final barrier between us. In the seconds to follow, we would long last be together. I reached for the iron latch and pushed. The door started open, and through the gap I saw him standing on the other side, illuminated by the gray glow spilling down through the opened window of a murder hole.

Thomas Gaius Thundre's eyes, blue the color and richness of sapphires and also his clan's kilt, captured mine. I recorded the rest of his magnificence from the periphery: dark hair, showing a trace of silver above both ears; his full beard on a face so handsome it nearly hurt to look upon him directly; his muscular torso clad in formfitting shirt; long, strong legs; big, booted feet, and that blue kilt. I caught his scent on my next gasp of breath—piney sweat, summer rain, and a hint of roses. For the hundredth time—*thousandth*?—I fell in love with him.

"Thunderheart," I said, and moved toward him.

The rush of happiness was brief. A shadow fell over him. The scent of roses and Thunderheart's sweat vanished, driven out by a fetor of swamps and cemeteries.

"You will never have him," said a deep, malevolent male voice.

The shadow drew back, and right before the door slammed, cutting me off from the man I loved, I saw that Thomas had degenerated to a skeleton, one still clad in his kilt. The skeleton reached its hand of bones toward me, pleading for my help.

Another thunderclap woke me, and I returned to the present in my bedroom, soaked in sweat and struggling to breathe. Music on low poured out of my cell phone's player—the end of that haunting old song from the 1980s sung by Sting. For a terrifying second, the skeleton stood in the shadows, half there between the shutter-clicks of blinks. I was convinced that if I reached out, I could grip his outstretched hand. But I hesitated, and the specter vanished, leaving me alone and haunted by my love for a man who'd died hundreds of years earlier and half a planet away.

***

My name is Jesse Sawyer, and I suppose it's true that I've always been different. Dating back for as long as I can remember, I've dreamed of the castle far from my home in Massachusetts and the handsome Scottish warrior who once lived there.

Thomas Gaius Thundre was real, and with his blessed sword Necravarian, fought beside Robert the Bruce during Scotland's First War of Independence against England. Known more to history by his epithet—Thunderheart—he was born on April the Fifteenth, 1306, at Castle Balglamis. Thomas was boyhood companion to Robert I, and joined the king at his side during his campaign to free Scotland. According to the *Itinerarium Perigrinorum et Gesta Regis Ricardi*, a Latin prose narrative from the time, *"Thomas was tall and of regal build, the color of his hair chestnut, his arms long and suited for wielding a sword, his long legs matched the rest of his body and marched him on toward victory."*

Unlike Robert the Bruce, Thomas suffered from a conspiracy of silence surrounding his sexuality. He was betrothed to marry Patrice Blatchely of a rival clan, but Thunderheart vanished before the union happened, and is believed to have been murdered by Lord Blatchely, her father, over rumors of infidelity with a male lover.

In an out of print hardcover, *Guide to the Abandoned United Kingdom*, on Page 113 is a grainy photograph of the remains of a castle located in remote Hintern-on-the-Bend, Scotland. A handful of ashlars—time-eroded gray stone blocks covered in lichen—are all that are left of the structure. The forest has grown in, and none of the castle's former grandeur is evident. But at night when I dream, I see it how it was, as though I've been to that castle in the flesh on numerous occasions, transported through time and the tempest of my heart's desires.

A lone painting of Thunderheart exists. It graces a wall in the British Museum's Medieval Art Gallery. I first saw the painting years before discovering it online and downloading it as wallpaper on my desktop; it was part of my very first dream of the warrior and his castle, and I've been drawing him in that same pose and others for as long as I've owned decent art supplies.

After the dream, I paced my rented loft apartment and looked out my window to an unobstructed view of the town's conservation woods. Thunderheart, reaching out to me for help through time and distance. I called up the image of the painting, creator unknown, and realized I'd gotten hard again. Choking down a dry swallow, I gazed into those unblinking twin sapphire eyes and lost my way, as has happened so often. I eased onto the sofa, a curbside rescue, and fell into a trance. I wasn't on the sofa but a bed with ornate carvings draped in royal blue blankets, not masturbating but being loved by the most noble of men. I wasn't in the present, a customer service wiz by day and artist on nights and weekends, but centuries in the past, my body beneath his, our bodies one.

"*Thomas*," I sighed, his name the most powerful fragment of a magic spell.

The painting jumped off the computer and into my

psyche. It renounced brooding dark strokes, tempura gold, and sapphire blue paint. Flesh tone became flesh. Love transformed him to three dimensions and conjured a beat from his heart. The thickness that entered my mouth first, my ass after his tongue licked it wet, was not that of a dream nor a ghost, but a living, breathing man.

I wrapped my arms around his sweating spine. "Stay," I begged.

Thunderheart opened his mouth, perhaps to pledge his promise of love and forever. I blinked, and time again robbed me of the one man, the only man, I have ever wanted. I was alone, on the verge of coming and only half there.

I tipped a glance at the computer. The painting stared back, pushing me past the edge. A cannonade of fireworks that only I could see erupted, consuming mind, body, soul. In the aftermath of the detonations, I huddled on the comfortable old sofa, naked and shivering as an early autumn breeze whispered through the room and gossiped over my skin.

And, upon that haunted wind, I imagined his voice, calling out to me for help. I spoke his name, giving voice to the magic, and pledged that I would save him.

***

I took an emergency leave of absence from work—a loved one in grave health, which wasn't so much a lie as a bending of the truth—and bought a ticket on the first available flight. I booked a shuttle to Logan Airport and, dressed in my trench coat and jeans and, traveling light, landed at Heath Row. With my copy of *Abandoned* in the backpack that also contained a fresh sketchpad and artist pencils, I departed for Hintern-on-the-Bend in a rental car and drove north, north.

A storm that had dogged my flight across half the Atlantic crept over England, turning the day dark. Eight hours later, a steady rain fell as I reached the rural outskirts of the hamlet. I had traveled new roads laid over old trails, the same course Thomas likely took upon his battles beside Robert the Bruce. I readied to make turns before the GPS told me to, as though aware of the way through that same kind of second sight.

The heavens opened up, and rain fell in sheets, making forward progress slow and dangerous. Still, I forged on, my heart hammering and my flesh electrified with excitement. Farms and cottages lit from within grew rare. The woods widened. I was close, so close.

When asked by my supervisor, I'd told a tall tale. I'd explained to airport security upon landing that I was an artist and student in London to see the Eight Mummies exhibit at the British Museum, among other historic works as part of my studies. I was thousands of miles from home and hundreds of kilometers from where I'd said I could be found on British soil, and none of the dangers modern or ancient, real or imaginary, mortal or supernatural, dared stop me from reaching my destination.

A pulse of prescient knowledge jolted me out of my thoughts and worries. I slammed on the brakes and pulled off to the side of the road. Nothing I saw told me I'd reached the next junction of my long voyage, but my inner eye knew I had arrived. I parked the car and locked it, pocketed the keys and my cell phone and, grabbing my backpack, I wandered into the storm and the darkening forest.

Rain cascaded. The Sitka spruce, Scots pine, sliver birch, and wych elm seemed to link branches, creating a living wall around me, guiding me in the only possible direction. I drank in the musky scent of the trees and land and agreed that I'd been here before, untold times, inhaling the same damp, woodsy smell until bewitched.

My heart raced. My cock swelled. Invisible electricity crackled over my skin. Closing my eyes and going on instinct, I walked forward, silently praying to whatever deity would listen that, while I was different, indeed a strange young man, I wasn't crazy.

I dug in my heels and opened my eyes. Phantoms surrounded me. I blinked, and the apparitions identified themselves as ashlars, the time-eroded stone blocks, all that remained of the ancient Castle Balglamis.

I froze. So, too, did time. The air thrummed with energy, elasticity. Seconds and centuries, eons and hours, minutes and millennia, interchanged. I tried to envision him—not the warrior in the painting but the man I knew from a lifetime of spectral love. Thomas Gaius Thundre was real. Maybe only real to me, a voice in my head challenged.

"No," I said aloud to the dark forest and castle ruins. More so, to myself.

I wandered forward and envisioned the places as I believed them once: the great hall within the embrasure opening in the parapet walls containing an oblong dining table and chairs *there*; the elegant wishbone archway beyond the portcullis and yett; the stone courtyard farther along; stables and gardens. Those landmarks weren't solid anymore, but I sensed them within reach, separated by time, which had become porous. Love had created a way through, and if I could reach that courtyard, I could also reach—

I blinked. Only desolation and dark woods met my eyes beyond the falling rain. The undercurrent faded. Time was solidifying again, reestablishing linear boundaries.

"*You can't have him,*" said the malevolent male voice.

I whirled. The image of a man dressed in black materialized. From somewhere unseen in the oppressive gloom, a crow cried out, sharp on the ear. Vileness crawled across my flesh. I steeled myself, though ready for what I couldn't say.

Not sure why, I said, "My love for him is stronger than your hatred!"

I was speaking from the heart. The figure drew back a step and the darkness brightened enough for me to see a pale glow flickering among the stone blocks. It welcomed me toward it and I found myself at the corner of an ashlar, where a climbing rose covered in thorns had produced a single blossom, the source of the glow. I leaned down and cupped the flower between my hands, inhaling deeply, recalling the fragrance of roses from my dream. I closed my eyes and conjured the warrior in my imagination.

"If you try to save him, I'll curse you, too," the figure in black warned.

"I'm already cursed," I said, "because Thomas and I are apart. Do your best."

I opened my eyes. Something long dead and decayed, rotting pieces held together within a cowled robe of rain-drenched crow feathers, staggered around the stone block and reached its withered hand toward me.

I gripped the flower, felt the sting of a thorn, and then the maddening rush of wind, currents, and colliding galaxies as space erupted in a repeat performance of the Big Bang that first gave life to the universe. Time came undone. I fell.

And fell.

***

Slowly, I surfaced from the abyss, and woke to a bright day far removed from the stormy landscape I'd been part of seemingly mere seconds earlier. I blinked and gasped for air. The damp and musty odor of the woods was gone, replaced by sunlight and the sweet smell of hay.

I sat up and found myself in a familiar courtyard. I turned. At my back the castle rose intact, its two halves joined by the wishbone arch. A dream, it had to be!

Only when I jumped to my feet, aware of the stones beneath my shoes, the illusion persisted, solidified. The castle wasn't a dream. Neither was the summer sky above it and the surrounding green landscape. A smile replaced the look of terror on my face. If the castle were whole once more, would its master be waiting for me? I wanted to believe it possible. My hand tingled from where the climbing rose had pricked my skin but when I looked, no wound bled.

As I wrestled with the memories of what I had seen and felt at the ruins, the steady clomp of hooves sounded at my back. Turning around took the greatest effort.

"Who—?" a man's voice called.

I faced him, aware of the wind rustling through the folds of my trench, feeling the sun-warmed stones of the courtyard through the soles of my shoes and the icy flicker of a true miracle passing through my blood, my bones— deeper, my *soul*.

The warrior stepped down from his steed. He wore the cobalt kilt I'd seen so often in my dreams, catching the breeze in a manner that suggested he controlled the elements.

"Thunderheart," I said.

Then gravity slammed into me, and the strength flowed out of my legs. I fell, and the warrior from my dreams caught me.

***

I had the sensation of levitating up, up, and was conscious of sunlight through slitted eyelids. But I didn't know if I was dreaming or awake. Perhaps, death had caught up to me, I mused, and I was being judged. Sent to Limbo, land of lost souls.

At one point untold minutes or millennia later, I opened my eyes. Sunlight showered down through an unshuttered window set in the blocks of ashlar. As the room around me swam into focus, I recognized bedclothes in a striking shade of sapphire blue, and the eyes of a man in a similar color, only far richer, far more beautiful, studying me. Thunderheart's eyes.

He moved beside the bed. A blade of moonlight-silver glinted against radiant sunlight. The swath appeared at my throat. I realized it was his sword, fabled Necravarian, and envisioned its sharp tip within an inch of my jugular. Fear ignited, replacing whatever else I'd felt until that moment.

"What manner of bewitchment is this?" he demanded, his voice bearing a soupcon of brogue. Before I could answer, he added, "Who are you?"

"I'm Jesse Sawyer," I managed. "And I don't know the exact bewitchment that brought me here to you, only that I'm sure magic was involved. There was a rose with a single flower, growing among the castle ruins."

The large hand on the hilt of the sword tightened. "Jesse Sawyer," said the handsome warrior. "I'm not sure why, but your name is as familiar as your face, like a dream that has haunted me for long years."

The blade drew back. Thunderheart choked down a heavy swallow that knotted his hairy throat, even that small thing attractive on him. Our glances met, held. I felt my lips smile first. Then my entire body joined in.

"I think it was the magic of love that made this possible," I offered, and sat up to my elbows.

"Love?"

I moved higher, aware of the bed's elegant carving, the sunlight and scent of the man before me. "You know who I am?"

Thunderheart nodded. "I believe I do, young Sawyer."

"I know you, Thomas. Thomas? Is it okay to call you by your first name? I've known you for as long as I've known myself, as though we're connected."

He considered my words without responding. Saying nothing, he stowed his broadsword—legendary Necravarian, reported to have been blessed by mystics and religious leaders alike—and moved toward me. My heart galloped. So tall and handsome, for a terrifying instant I feared him as much as I desired him. I willed my pulse to steady and reminded myself that I trusted him. I loved him.

Thomas leaned down and caressed my cheek with a gentleness hands of his size normally weren't capable of. "Jesse Sawyer," he growled.

The sparest of smiles widened. And then he kissed me.

***

We fumbled awkwardly with one another's clothes— me, with kilt and boots from a time so long before my own, he with buttons, zippers, and laces crafted in a time far in the future.

"Here, like this," I gasped between kisses.

After Thomas had stripped me bare, he stood back and studied my body. His cock, so thick and magnificent, jutted up from his thick pelt of pubic hair, signaling his approval. "*Beautiful*," he sighed.

I boldly took the warrior's cock in my hand and tested its uncircumcised head with my lips. I breathed in his scent, sucked on his erection, and tasted the gamy drops of nectar that leaked out, proof of his excitement. I fondled Thomas's meaty balls, sensing from so many past fantasies in a future world that he would approve. He did, and rose to the tops of his toes, a look of relief mixed with joy painted brightly on his face.

"Long last," he said. "You have escaped my dreams and are here, in the flesh."

He guided my face off his cock and pulled me back to my feet. The scrape of his beard on my face sent icy-hot pinpricks cascading over my epidermis in concentric ripples. Our cocks ground together. I pulled on his balls, fearing I might climax from his kiss alone.

A forceful shove onto the bed of blue blankets, and then I was on my stomach, being licked, devoured. The knight's facial hair wove even more powerful magic while he feasted upon my ass. Finger followed tongue. Cock soon replaced finger, and I thought I would go mad from the pressure.

"Yes," I moaned into the bedclothes.

Thomas leaned over me, his front bracing my spine. His breath rained warmth across my neck. His thickness inside me completed the incantation and fulfilled all that was missing from the spell. Linked together, we were both whole now, a kind of male Yin-yang. The pain of having his cock inside me became pleasurable. I mentally recorded the hair on his legs, stretched protectively against mine, his big, bare feet, the weight of his balls, the prickle on his cheek.

"I love you," I gasped.

"And I you, Jesse."

He drew back so that just the head of his cock remained within me. Then he thrust in, and only his balls stopped him from going deeper. I moaned my approval. The warrior kissed me, fucked me, loved me.

At one point in our lovemaking, a flutter of wings and shadows drew my gaze up to the unshuttered window. A crow had landed on the stone sill and stood watching us. I called out Thomas's name. The crow flew away.

***

He lay atop the bed, one bare leg and foot extended out from the covers. Sunlight embossed his face and chest. In that moment as I sketched him, the universe loved Thunderheart almost as much as I did.

"Tell me more," he said. My blood surged at the sound of his voice, no longer talking only in my head. "About your world and this link forged between us."

I ceased sketching and shared details of a future where men set foot on the moon but still fought over the most ridiculous of differences. "As far as us, I don't know. But for as long as I can remember, there's only been you."

He reclined, the rise and fall of his hair-covered chest

hypnotic. "So far from Scotland…there were nights as we fought the English when dreams of you saved me from despair. I believed in our fight, because I believed in you."

Silence fell over the keep, and words no longer became necessary. Thomas licked his lips, and I ached for his kisses.

"This future world of yours," he began.

"Is loud and dirty, and magic is harder to find there," I said. "It's a world mostly without heart."

"And how is it we're able to understand one another, you and I? I speak the Gaelic—and yet talking with you is effortless."

I hadn't thought about that particular twist among the many that had occurred since my arrival to the castle ruins. "Magic?"

"Or one of these enlightened miracles you've told me of—like the ability to cross oceans, to fly, and to travel as high in the sky as the moon. I'm intrigued by your world," said Thomas. "Any world with you in it."

I set down my pencil, placed my hand on his hairy ankle, and caressed my way to his toes. Lust for him again consumed me. "I'm here now, with you in your world. So long as we're together, I'm happy."

A shadow passed over the knight's expression, and again I remembered the dream, the skeleton. Thomas slipped fully out from beneath the covers and stood before the window dressed only in golden dapples of sunlight.

"Thomas?" I asked.

He tipped a wounded look my way. "I would go if we could return to your time, Jesse."

"Why?"

"You talk of this dark sorcerer, the warlock dressed in black. Since my return to Castle Balglamis, I've felt the darkness coming closer, coming for me. Lord Blatchely of the Fitzcammon Clan…even now, he draws nearer to this castle."

"Blatchely," I parroted. The lone word tasted foul upon my tongue. "Thomas, according to history, after his visit to seal your union with his daughter…"

My voice trailed to a whisper. History, Fate, the Gods—whatever power granted my travel back through time had seen fit to return me to this pivotal moment.

"We have to leave, Thomas," I said.

"And go where?"

As much as it saddened me, I knew we couldn't remain in the castle. My eyes drifted over his magnificent physique to the day beyond the window. Gray tendrils crept across the horizon. Soon, the clouds would block the sun. I moved beside Thomas and melted into his embrace. Our eyes met, held, and the passion I felt for him was returned in equal doses, telegraphed by sunlight.

"Away from this place," I said.

Thomas leaned down to kiss me. "Gather your things," he said when we parted. "For away, then, we must. Away *together*."

I started toward the bed. He held onto my wrist, turned me back, and captured me with eyes the color of jay feathers, delphiniums, and precious sapphire gemstones.

"Together," I repeated.

Thomas released me, and I hastily began to dress, pulling on socks, underwear, and jeans. I gathered my art supplies and was lacing up my shoes when the cadence of multiple hooves trampling over earth reached us through breaks in the castle's wall.

***

Lord Blatchely came striding toward Thunderheart's castle on the back of a black steed whose decorative crests bore the image of a crow.

"Godspeed, Jesse," Thomas said. "Quickly, to the postern."

We hurried down the keep's staircase, through the great hall, toward what amounted to the castle's back door. A thunderous knock sounded on the slab of oak at the front. Thunderheart drew Necravarian, seized hold of my wrist, and pulled me after him, shielding my body with his. At the postern, I found myself reliving the dream I'd experienced so many times—the two of us, about to be separated as forces of evil moved in, keeping us apart.

Thomas released me to undo the iron bolt, and my panic intensified. This was when I would lose him, I was certain. The door flew open, showing a gray afternoon devoid of sunlight. I followed Thomas outside, trusting in him and in our love.

We hadn't gone far in the direction of the stables when an abomination beat enormous black wings at my face, knocking me to the ground. One moment, it was a bird. I blinked, and the crow-thing melted, reformed, into the upright form of a man in a black cowled robe. A smell of swamps assailed my senses.

"*Blatchely*," said Thomas.

The man in black's cruel face focused from the warrior to me. "Curious," he said.

Soldiers dressed in dark kilts swarmed around the castle's walls and surrounded us. I rose up from the ground only to be shoved back down.

"By what authority does your clan justify such aggressions here on my clan's soil?" Thomas demanded.

The sorcerer flashed a frigid grin, the gesture more snarl than actual smile. "You were to have prepared for a wedding, Thundre. *Thunderheart*," Blatchely spat. "Instead, I find you with this…squire? Lover?"

Blatchely's eyes narrowed upon me, and I sensed his consciousness worming around in my thoughts.

I know you, he said, though his lips never moved. *Somehow, we've met before. No…after!*

I shook my head in an attempt to block him out. A crow's voice shrieked, right beside my ear, the pain so brilliant I felt my senses surrendering. Then Thomas called out my name, and the world swam back into focus. I looked over to see him struggling against the dark soldiers holding him down on his knees. The sorcerer's men had disarmed him of Necravarian. The sky swam far above my eyes, ominous and gray, the heavens poised to open up, just like in the future time I'd left to rescue the man I loved from history's clutches. I'd squandered the miracle I'd been granted.

A lone drop of rain pelted my cheek. A pale glow teased my vision at the periphery. I broke focus with Thomas and tipped a look toward the castle's wall, where a climbing rose scaled the gray stone blocks. Surely, it was the same mystical entity from my future! Two roses were in bloom among the thorns.

"Now, I understand," said Blatchely, drawing my gaze back to him. "You and this pup…a conspiracy of silence born of unnatural acts between two men!"

"You're the only unnatural thing here," I said, and reached into my pocket.

A quick finger shuffle through my phone, and music blasted out—Sting, in the middle of singing about fortresses built around hearts. The outburst stunned the guards and even their master. Thomas threw back their arms, jumped to his feet, and quickly bested the soldier in possession of Necravarian with a punch to the man's chin. In one fluid motion, he swung the broadsword, and its tip was pressed against Blatchely's throat. Thomas waved his free hand, signaling caution. The dark soldiers froze.

"I should kill you now, Blatchely," Thomas said.

Blatchely's grin returned. "You cannot escape me. I have allies and servants from Scotland to England who'll see to it that you suffer, Thundre. You, and your young male lover."

"I don't think so," I said. "Thomas, we're leaving."

He glanced my way, and our eyes met. "The future?"

"It will be a better one with you in it," I said, and reached toward the castle wall.

I plucked the two roses from the climbing vine. The sensation of time's porousness again teased my skin, a warning that we needed to move with haste. A single, final chance, for time was solidifying.

As I hurried toward Thomas, Blatchely tossed up his arms and shifted shape. The giant crow soared toward me and stole one of the blossoms from my grasp. The world I'd been transported back to began to ripple out of focus.

Thomas reached toward me. "Jesse!"

Another second, and I would lose him forever.

This time, I grabbed hold of his hand and held on. The universe came apart in an eruption of light and heat. Then, there was only darkness.

***

I woke on the ground, damp and shivering. Rain spilled down from a sky filled with shadows. I stood and wiped my eyes. The phantoms around me focused into the ancient stone blocks, all that remained of the castle. I was back in the present.

I spun around, seemingly alone. "*Thomas*," I called.

The warrior didn't answer. A throaty, malevolent chuckle, however, did. "I told you I would curse you if you attempted to save him," said the rotting effigy of Lord Blatchely.

The corpse moved toward me, its skeletal hands outstretched. Then Blatchely split in two as Necravarian sliced the sorcerer down the middle. The halves dissolved, and Thomas stood before me, his fabled broadsword clutched in both hands.

"Jesse," he said and drew me tightly against him.

I hugged Thomas back. "You're here. You're alive!"

"You saved me, and now we are one in your world."

My world. There were so many details yet to face, but as our lips crushed together, Thomas claiming me as his, we were together, and in all the universe, it was all that mattered.

If you loved this anthology,
please leave a review!

MORE ABOUT
SINCYR PUBLISHING

At SinCyr Publishing, we wish to provide relatable characters facing real problems to our readers, in the sexiest or most romantic manner possible. Our intent is to offer a large selection of books to readers that cover topics ranging from sexual healing to sexual empowerment, to body positivity, gender equality, and more.

Too many of us experience body shaming, sexual shaming, and/or sexual abuse in our lives and we want to publish stories that allow people to connect to the characters and find healing. This means showing healthy BDSM practices, characters that understand consent and proper communication, characters that stare down toxic culture and refuse to take part... No matter what the content is, our focus is on empowering our readers through our books.